PRAISE FOR ACCELERATED GROWTH ENVIRONMENT

"A sapphic eco-thriller perfect for fans of Becky Chambers and Martha Wells."

REBECCA ROANHORSE, NEW YORK TIMES BESTSELLING AUTHOR OF THE AWARD-WINNING SERIES "BETWEEN EARTH AND SKY"

"High-tech, high-ecology, and high-tension family and work relationships all combine in a stunning new story from Lauren C. Teffeau. This adventure for humanity's future survival will win your heart and your mind!"

FRAN WILDE, AWARD-WINNING AUTHOR OF "A PHILOSOPHY OF THIEVES"

"This gripping eco-mystery is a page turner with a no-nonsense romantic interest, a lovable robot companion, and an extraordinary solarpunk setting."

SARENA ULIBARRI, AWARD-WINNING AUTHOR OF "ANOTHER LIFE"

"Anyone who says there is no romance in science has never read Lauren C. Teffeau's stories. And I don't just mean the kissy-face kind of romance, I mean that soul-deep longing for understanding and connection to other people and the world we all inhabit. Let this be the future you imagine and work toward building, dear reader."

CURTIS C. CHEN, BESTSELLING AUTHOR OF "TRUE BLUE KANGAROO"

ALSO BY LAUREN C. TEFFEAU

A Hunger With No Name (2024)

Implanted (2018)

ACCELERATED GROWTH ENVIRONMENT

LAUREN C. TEFFEAU

Published by Shiraki Press
Mill Creek, Washington, USA
First edition 2026

 For information about this book, including distribution and media reviews, scan or visit:

shirakipress.com/books/accelerated-growth-environment/

ACCELERATED GROWTH ENVIRONMENT
Copyright © 2026 by Lauren C. Teffeau
All rights reserved.

ISBN: 978-1-970458-02-2 (Paperback)
ISBN: 978-1-970458-00-8 (EPUB)

Library of Congress Control Number: 2026935302

This book is a work of fiction. Names, characters, organizations, places, and events are products of the author's imagination, or are used fictitiously. Any resemblance to actual persons, living or dead, is entirely coincidental.

NO PART OF THIS BOOK MAY BE USED OR REPRODUCED TO TRAIN ARTIFICIAL INTELLIGENCE SYSTEMS.

Published by Shiraki Press
P.O. Box 13394, Mill Creek, WA 98082
shirakipress.com

To everyone working toward a brighter future.
Don't forget to stop and smell the tiger lilies.

1

THE POLLINATOR DRONE needed to be put out of its misery.

Horrid squeals from the rotors accompanied the erratic contortions of the tendril-like injectors as it flopped about on the ground like a beached squid. It had already kicked up enough dirt to cover the fronds of the nearby century plants in a fine powder.

Dr. Jorna Benton fiddled with the helmet of her biosuit to block out the drone's mechanical howls. "Better get Meigs over here," she told the genderless, child-sized automaton at her side.

Dust dulled the Savvy-3000's matte silver casing. Its illuminated eyes flashed when it finished its task. "Chief Engineer Samantha Meigs is on her way, Dr. Benton."

"Thanks, Savvy."

Jorna settled in to wait on a boulder overlooking long

rows of yucca, lavender, and flowering cacti, still unused to having the habitat all to herself for a change. If she closed her eyes and pulled the scent of piñon pine and sage her suit couldn't filter out deep into her lungs, she could imagine she was back in southern Colorado.

But the similarities ended as soon as she looked out across the desert tier. The Climasphere was a remarkable, human-made ecosystem, capturing nearly every natural region on Earth within its walls as it traversed the Atlantic. Dozens of different biomes crawled up the sides of the circular habitat like super-sized stadium bleachers oriented around a pitch. Except in this case, the pitch was actually a small stretch of ocean.

With the spangled sunlight filtering through the solar mesh of the dome that encased the habitat, Jorna could almost forget about the sheer artificiality of it all, it was so beautiful.

A metallic glint caught her eye near the hangar, carved right into the sides of Tiers 2 and 3. That would be Meigs on one of the air skiffs.

Jorna sighed. This was taking a lot longer than she expected, and Meigs was still about ten minutes out. Jorna's assistant had already gone into standby mode, but the automaton flashed to life when she addressed it. "Savvy, visual of Tier 7, Quadrant 3, please." Might as well stay busy while they waited.

"Incoming, Dr. Benton."

On Jorna's touchscreen, an overhead view of this portion of the high desert tier appeared thanks to one of the monitoring drones buzzing around. Species names overlaid the different plots as Jorna scrolled across the camera feed, but she didn't need the prompts at this point. "Looks like two rows of desert willows are struggling after being transplanted from the Tree Farm. Send out a diagnostic request for specimens starting with number HD-144 through HD-172 to see why they're showing signs of stress."

"Acknowledged, Dr. Benton." Savvy was a lifesaver, maintaining a log of all Jorna's decisions needed to keep such an incredible cross-section of plants thriving.

"We'll need to plant replacement specimens from the Tree Farm for the ones that can't be salvaged, pulling more seeds from the vault as necessary."

"Acknowledged."

Some die-off was to be expected after the Climasphere's first harvest, but rewilding a significant portion of Earth was a huge, multi-year commitment. She didn't want to burn through their reserves too early. At the moment, they were still well within tolerances, but it was something to monitor going forward. Nothing could go wrong on her watch.

And nothing would—the same pledge she'd made to the selection committee well over a year ago now. She'd make sure of it.

The hum of the skiff's repulsor lifts heralded the arrival of the chief engineer. Just in time too. Jorna's shoulders were already locked with tension from cycling through different contingencies, all of them ranging from less than ideal to catastrophically bad.

Jorna waved as Meigs maneuvered the air skiff over to where Jorna waited. "Came across it on my rounds this morning," she called out as the engineer hopped off the skiff. "It's not responding to network commands."

Meigs frowned down at the malfunctioning drone. Underneath her helmet, her gray-blond hair was shoved back from her pale face in a fraying braid, and grease streaked the front of her suit. "Good thing we aren't any higher," she said with a critical look around the tier.

She was right. Any farther up the inner wall of the Climasphere, they'd need to deploy extra scrubbers to clean the particulates the drone sent flying before they fouled the habitat's delicate ecosystem. They'd already found out the hard way how pollen from the taiga evergreens growing on Tier 8 could form a concrete-like film on the inner dome thanks to the air circulators, gumming up the place for days.

"We lucked out for once," Jorna said.

Meigs snorted. "Always something, isn't there." She shrugged off her pack and rifled through her collection of magna-drivers, pliers, spanners, and random electrical components until her gloved hands closed over a remote restrainer. With the click of a button, she signaled the drone to power down, finally putting an end to its death squeals. "We could've brought actual pollinators along, but *no*. We're stuck with these robot monstrosities."

"I've always thought they're kinda cool, the way they dart through the air like some kind of jellyfish, casting down their tentacles to pollinate the plants," Jorna offered.

Meigs grunted as she popped off the panel protecting the drone's CPU and attached a diagnostic lead. "Just some freaking bees, Jorna. That's all I'm asking for." She pulled up the troubleshooting menu on her touchscreen.

"What you're asking for is even more chaos in our closed

little system. You can jerry-rig just about anything, but even you couldn't ensure a swarm wouldn't find its way into the air ducts, or worse. Drones are far more predictable—and accurate—compared to the real thing."

"Sure. *If* they're working properly."

"Then it's a good thing I have you."

Meigs waved her off and returned her attention to the screen. "And I have a to-do list a mile long without worrying about another malfunctioning robot. Piece of shit." She yanked the diagnostic cable off the drone with a scowl then tipped her head toward Savvy. "With apologies to present company."

"No apology is necessary, Chief Engineer Samantha Meigs. I am an AI assistant, not a horticulture drone. We bear no resemblance beyond a small percentage of our circuitry sourced from the same microchip production facility."

Jorna grinned at Meigs's frustrated groan. "Never mind her, Savvy. Meigs just likes to complain."

The engineer shoved her middle finger in Jorna's direction as she poked through the drone's innards. Something sparked in the drone's CPU cavity, deepening her scowl. "I've earned the right to complain after spending the last week cleaning up the mess the horticulture techs left behind after the harvest."

"We were all pretty beat, and clearly some things—a *lot* of things," Jorna revised at the grim expression on the engineer's face, "fell by the wayside. But I'm chalking a lot of this up to it being our first go-round. Things will be easier next time."

Meigs just grunted. "It better."

Jorna couldn't blame Meigs for feeling doubtful. The harvest had taken a toll not only on the personnel but also on the drones and other equipment. When Meigs wasn't monitoring the Climasphere's essential systems, she was troubleshooting the drones or running the fabber to replace equipment that had already failed or depreciated to such an extent it was no longer useful. It took a unique type of person to excel at such exacting work, which Meigs was, even if it came bundled with endless complaints and a somewhat taciturn personality.

Not that Jorna could say she was any better. More than once she'd ended up spending the night in the Tree Farm or her lab instead of making her way back to her quarters, so focused on her research and keeping things running smoothly, everything else got short shrift.

"Come on," Jorna said. "It isn't all bad. With the techs on break, I can finally hear my own thoughts again."

Was that a grin beneath Meigs's helmet? "And I thought I was the antisocial one."

Now it was Jorna's turn to smile. "Nope. I'm just better at hiding it."

"What other secrets are you hiding, Doc?"

It was a joke, but Jorna still had to force back the knee-jerk paranoia she'd lived with so long it only elicited a distant pang when she said, "None that I'm sharing with you."

Meigs's cackle devolved into muttered curses as she continued her inspection of the drone.

Savvy stirred in the periphery. "Dr. Benton, incoming message from Commander Kaysar."

That pulled Jorna up short. "Tell her I'm busy at the

moment." Though that excuse wouldn't deter someone like the commander for long.

Meigs glanced up from the drone. "If you need to take that, don't mind me."

"It's fine. Besides, we're in the middle of this."

"*Sure.*" Meigs suddenly sat back on her haunches and cast Jorna a speculative look. "Any problems I need to know about?"

"What? No." The level of professionalism on board the Climasphere was insanely high, no doubt because so many of them believed so strongly in their mission, they didn't have time to indulge in petty turf wars. "Why do you say that?"

Meigs shrugged as she unscrewed a panel protecting the drone's circuitry. "It's just you get kind of jumpy whenever the commander's mentioned."

How had Meigs put that together? No, it didn't matter, Jorna told herself. It couldn't. "I don't know what you mean."

"Well, there was that one staff meeting when she came over to say hello and—"

Jorna well remembered how the commander had snuck up behind her. "She startled me, that's all."

Meigs snapped the panel back in place and gave her a look, brows raised. "You glared into your touchscreen the rest of the meeting."

"That's because I spilled hot tea down the front of my shirt thanks to her." Jorna's embarrassment had warred with her discomfort as the tea cooled and the wet fabric grew chill. It hadn't helped she'd been seated underneath one of the air vents.

"Hmm," Meigs said, unconvinced. "Just the other day you nearly jumped out of your skin when Kaysar brushed the dirt off your suit after our fight with the load of cypress trees, remember?"

Jorna did. The commander had come to oversee the loading of the last transports. Jorna had been too busy to notice, but once she'd taken a step back, the commander was suddenly in front of her, asking for an update. Jorna stammered through her response as the commander's hands drifted along her arms and shoulders, swiping away the soil that had accumulated in the seams of Jorna's suit. The hectic loading platform receded into the background for a brief moment at the feeling of being taken care of for a change instead of always doing the caretaking. Of the plants. Of her horticulture techs. She'd been so very tired from the harvest, she'd nearly forgotten herself and her responsibilities.

Her cheeks heated. And now it was happening again. "I'm lucky I still knew my name by the time the cypress shipped," Jorna said as dismissively as she could.

"If I didn't know any better…" Meigs pursed her lips, seemingly uncertain whether she wanted to give voice to what she was thinking. "You know, I can see the appeal." She grinned down at the busted drone. "A woman who knows what she wants and is respected enough to get it. I mean, she joined Earth Shield after her stint in the Navy and she *still* got this job."

For decades, Earth Shield had been known for its aggressive efforts to raise awareness of environmental problems and punish bad actors by any means necessary. Kaysar had been the one to position the organization to become a division of the Climate Corps now that the political will to tackle these issues was finally ascendant.

A remarkable transformation by any metric.

Meigs shook her head. "I guess when you make eco-terrorism outfits go legit, you can do what you want."

The tension was back in Jorna's shoulders. She wanted to deny it, but the engineer was far too perceptive for that. Damage control was the best she could hope for. "Not another word, Meigs. I mean it."

"I'm right, aren't I?" Meigs let out a low whistle.

Jorna crossed her arms. "That's it. I'm going to write you up for noncompliance."

Meigs snorted at the empty threat. "Come on. I deserve a commendation for figuring it out."

Savvy flashed beside Jorna. "Dr. Benton, query. How should I characterize Chief Engineer Meigs's infraction for her work record?"

A strangled chuckle escaped her. "Disregard, Savvy. It was a joke." She gave Meigs a sharp look. "Isn't that right?"

The engineer's shoulders silently shook as she held up her hands in truce. Then she went back to reading through the drone diagnostics on her touchscreen.

"So what's the damage?" Jorna asked, eager for a new topic, one rooted in facts and not speculation that was far too close to the truth.

Meigs sighed, thankfully back to business. "Looks like there's a defect with one of the internal rotors. Probably got fatigued with all the new planting we've been doing."

That fell into the less-than-ideal category. "Could that be an issue with the other horticulture drones?"

She grimaced. "Could be for the ones with the same lot

number for that particular part."

Jorna forced back a curse. Just their luck to discover the issue now when they were shorthanded. "For all I know, that could be all of them, Meigs."

The Climasphere had been built at sea from the Philadelphia shipyard over the course of the last four years. Like a lodestone, the project had drawn some of the best and brightest from around the world to create a habitat that could produce enough plant matter to seed a new future. The drones alone needed to support the twenty thousand-plus hectares of growing space were in the thousands, ordered in massive quantities to minimize transportation costs.

Meigs waved her off. "I'll get it sorted."

"And when you're done, I'll need a full accounting of all affected drones." If Jorna couldn't rely on the drones to pollinate their share of plants, that would affect the next harvest and by extension the milestones they needed to hit to put off even more catastrophic warming. Delays, setbacks... *failure*. Her lungs squeezed at all the implications.

"Two days, max," Meigs promised as she hefted the drone and placed it on board her skiff.

"After that I want you to expand your analysis to the others. The augers, the spot irrigators, the—"

"I'll handle it, Doc. Don't worry."

Worry was what Jorna's job description essentially boiled down to as the Climasphere's principal scientist. But she didn't say that. She just sucked in a deep breath as the chief engineer scrambled onto the skiff.

Meigs tossed down another remote restraining device.

"Here. In case you run into another malfunctioning drone. Have Savvy drop them off at the Hive." They were programmed to return to the storage bay when they were low on power or there was some kind of error, but clearly that wasn't a failsafe.

Jorna saluted her with the restrainer. "Will do." As Meigs headed out, she turned to Savvy. "Schedule the next available pollinator drone to tackle this section. There's only a short window of time for those cactus flowers."

"Acknowledged."

Jorna had Savvy summon their skiff, docked at the far end of the quadrant, and they were soon underway, getting on with her rounds. With the broken drone finally silenced, Meigs gone, and Savvy in standby, peace had once again returned to the habitat. Only a week ago, the sphere's exterior hangar doors had been wide open as countless transports zoomed in and out and about, loaded down with specimens dozens of countries were reliant upon to rebuild and remediate their territories from fire and warfare, drought and mass die-offs. Two similar structures were stationed in the Pacific, and another was in the process of being built in the Indian Ocean. The Climaspheres were intended to symbolize a new era of cooperative effort to claw back whatever they could under the aegis of the United Nations' Climate Action Council.

And it was *working*, thanks to Jorna and a legion of horticulture techs. The modified plant strains had flourished in the Climasphere's accelerated growth environment. Advances in electroculture techniques sped up the germination and maturation of specimens so they'd be ready to transplant in a fraction of the time compared to conventional methods. When they reached their first stop off the coast of South Carolina, their plants were shipped off to shore up low country waterways at risk of even further erosion, infuse dying forests with more resilient varieties, and provide farms with drought-tolerant strains of cotton, corn, soybeans, and rice. Plants that would make a difference for years to come. But now that the inaugural harvest was over, all that was left was the hard work of preparing for the next one in six months.

A slushy sleet was falling by the time she and Savvy reached Tier 5. The Climasphere could mimic the water cycle on Earth to an uncanny degree. Great for the plants. Not so great for her. Her biosuit had built-in voltage protection, but she wasn't about to test that today, not with the electroculture gradient running through each tier to spur on plant growth.

She parked the skiff over the temperate forest tier, just skimming the tops of the tallest deciduous specimens in Quadrant 1. The chipset embedded in her helmet's visor allowed her to take stock of which plants needed to be replaced as she panned across the tier. "We'll need ten more birch trees in plot seven, Savvy."

"Acknowledged." Savvy tilted its head. "Dr. Benton, another incoming message from the commander."

Jorna had almost succeeded in pushing it out of her mind entirely. Only the soft slap and patter of sleet against her helmet sounded over the buzzing in her ears. She heaved a sigh. No mistakes. Isn't that what she promised herself? She couldn't avoid Kaysar forever. "Put it through, Savvy."

2

"CHANNEL OPEN," SAVVY announced.

"Dr. Benton, I thought for sure you'd refuse me like you have every other time since the harvest." The gregarious nature of Commander Ava Kaysar came through the transmission so clearly, it was almost like she was standing beside Jorna, an irrepressible grin on her face, instead of her post on the Bridge. "But I'm glad to see I was wrong."

"You know how much I enjoy proving you wrong," Jorna replied as blandly as she could, and still earned a delighted laugh from the commander. "But it's true we've been buried over here. How can I help you?"

"You're scheduled for a checkup with Dr. Rafa this afternoon, are you not?"

Of course the commander knew about her checkup. She knew *everything* that went on in the Climasphere. "Err... Yes."

"Good. After that, I was hoping you would join me for dinner in my quarters this evening."

A strangled breath escaped Jorna. This was it.

"Now don't say no before you've even heard me out," the commander went on.

"I wouldn't dream of it," Jorna managed to say.

"There's something we're overdue to discuss."

Cold slicked down Jorna's spine as though the falling sleet had infiltrated her suit. *Overdue* was putting it mildly, but that hadn't kept her from hoping they would never have to address it. No such luck. She couldn't say no, and she was certain they both knew it. "Acknowledged. Benton, out."

An abrupt way to end the call, but she didn't dare say anything else until... What? She didn't have a playbook for what came next, and that was almost as embarrassing as her faux pas that kicked off this whole mess, on the eve of the launch no less.

Jorna stared down at the tier without actually looking at the trees. She'd known this day was coming. Heading things off before they got any worse would have been the smart, sensible thing to do. But instead she'd ignored it, buried herself in her work so she'd never have to deal with it. And if Meigs was any indication, Jorna had done a pretty poor job of it.

Mistake.

Like a process running in the background she was afraid to shut down, fearing the effect on the rest of the system. One she'd put off for so long, it was now time for a huge software update, no matter how inconvenient.

She whirled around, momentarily thrown to find Savvy

watching her more carefully than usual. "We're heading back." She stepped up to the skiff's controls and took a deep breath. Instead of following the curving tiers like she normally did, she pointed it directly toward the hangar and cut across the circular sea churning below, doing her best to avert her gaze from all that blue.

"Dr. Benton, query."

Jorna's hands tightened over the steering wheel. She glanced over at the automaton and found it still watching her closely. "What is it, Savvy?"

"Is something bothering you?"

She faced forward once more. "I don't know what you mean."

"Your heart rate and respiration levels have increased, and you are pushing the limits of the skiff's speed."

Jorna immediately backed off the accelerator. "Sorry. Guess I just wasn't paying attention."

"You've been in this heightened state since your conversation with the commander."

Jorna grit her teeth. Savvy was programmed to interpret non-verbals and a whole host of biofeedback markers to aid Jorna in her work. And Savvy was curious, more so than any other AI assistant she'd worked with previously. Access to the latest tech was one of the perks of the job. Supposedly.

"What topic does she want to talk to you about?"

"I have no idea." Denial. Lying to Savvy was a new low for her, particularly since she wasn't fooling anyone. Or anything.

"Query—"

"Get Meigs on the line, would you?" Distraction.

"One moment. Channel open."

Before Jorna could say anything, Meigs broke in with, "Don't start with me, Benton. I said two days."

"That's not why I called. I'll be meeting with the commander later on—"

"Oh, *really*? How interesting."

Damn it all. Jorna counted tiers to keep from snapping at Meigs. "As I was saying, I'll see if she can spare some of her techs to support you. Help take some of the pressure off, you know?"

There was silence on the line for a brief moment, then Meigs sighed in frustration. "Don't bother if I'm just going to have to train them on the drone specs."

"I'll see what I can do," Jorna said flatly before disconnecting.

Of course Meigs couldn't simply accept help—it had to be on her terms or not at all. Even if the commander's techs could only hotwire door controls, it was better than nothing. Not that Jorna was about to tell Meigs that. The chief engineer knew what her responsibilities were—all Jorna could do was provide what resources she could and then stay the hell out of the way.

The skiff approached the electrostatic field that kept the habitat as pristine as possible. It sizzled off just as the skiff was inches away from entering the hangar then hummed back to life as they passed through. The hairs on the back of her neck still stood on end as she maneuvered the skiff toward one of the empty slips. The docking clamps locked on and brought it in the rest of the way. Jorna disembarked and trotted down the metal gangway, Savvy lumbering a few feet behind her. There, she stripped out of her biosuit and placed it on one of the hooks for her next foray into the habitat.

The humidity that had built up in her suit was quickly replaced by the slick chill of the mechanical corridor leading to her uncharacteristically messy laboratory. The harvest had taken up her bandwidth for so long, tidying things up in here had fallen way down on the list of priorities. Data sticks, too many of them unlabeled. Plastipaper printouts of journal articles featuring the latest research in horticulture and plant genomics marked up in her crabbed writing. A week's worth of mugs half-full of cold tea. All of it cluttered various surfaces around the room. At least no one was around to see it, and Meigs and Savvy didn't count.

Though somehow the place seemed even messier than usual today. Her fingers itched to clean it up, but if she gave in now she'd never make it to her medical appointment in time.

Savvy went over to its charging station, and as the cage came down, it announced, "Transplant requests from the Tree Farm have been finalized. I took the liberty of drafting a planting schedule for the coastal tier for you to review for implementation as early as tomorrow. Results from the gene variation analysis for angiosperms in an accelerated growth environment have been recorded to the experiment file directory. You've asked me to remind you to respond to Danika Sutcliffe-Xi's message. Do you wish to dismiss this reminder as you have thirty-one times previously?"

Jorna looked up from the stack of papers she was sorting through. Savvy's eyes blinked slowly as it waited for her response to its unusually pointed question. "You haven't downloaded new management software from the database by any chance, have you?"

Savvy's eyes flashed. "You are correct, Dr. Benton. I have updated myself with an advanced social control program to help me support you in all things." The standard AI directive, augmented by programs capturing the latest productivity hacks and psychological insights to customize its approach.

"In other words, passive-aggressive people management? I broke up with one of my partners over that kind of bullshit, you know." And her own family before that, she thought grimly.

Savvy's eyes opened wide in imitation of concern. "Apologies, Dr. Benton, but when my previous reminders went unheeded, I thought it best to modify my approach. If you would like me to refrain from using this methodology, I will do so."

Jorna massaged her eyelids. She understood Savvy's perplexion and why it sought out a different way of "helping" her work. But this wasn't something that could be out-logicked, as it was entirely too human. "I have low tolerance for manipulation. Make sure you balance the outcome probabilities of this particular method with the absolute certainty it's just going to piss me off."

It blinked slowly as it processed that. "So noted, Dr. Benton."

She sighed. "And delete that notification. I will not be writing Danika now or ever. If I haven't come up with anything to say at this point, then nothing more needs to be said."

"So noted, Dr. Benton. Query: Why does that decision

make you"—it cocked its head to the side—"upset?"

Savvy, knowingly or not, seemed determined to rifle through *all* of Jorna's old baggage today.

"Because it's just a reminder I left her behind to go on this mission."

"She didn't want to come?" Immediate family over the age of eighteen and in good health would have been given training for a job somewhere on the sphere, but...

Jorna grimaced. "More like I didn't want her here." It sounded terrible out loud, but it was the truth. If she had brought Danika along, they would have grown to regret it, even if Danika couldn't admit that when Jorna broke the news to her.

"So noted, Dr. Benton. Query: Why did you decide that, given how solitary this mission is? Wouldn't she have brought you companionship?"

Jorna blew out a breath. Sometimes Savvy took its directives way too seriously.

The Savvy-3000's inherent curiosity was one of the series's selling points. In order for Jorna to get the full benefit from using the AI assistant, she was supposed to answer its questions to improve Savvy's profile of her, but explaining to a robot the difference between convenience and companionship seemed a bit much.

Savvy's illuminated eyes hadn't left her face. Jorna cleared her throat. "You know better than anyone the extent of my responsibilities on the Climasphere. The cost of that companionship would have been too high."

Danika would have expected things from Jorna she couldn't give. Danika already resented all the time Jorna had put into her training for the mission because their relationship was no longer a "priority." When Danika started talking about the expedition like they were about to embark on a seven-year cruise instead of a mission crucial to restoring the Earth, her enthusiasm created a pressure in Jorna's chest that only grew bigger and bigger, like a balloon, until it popped when she realized it just wasn't going to work. So she decided to cut Danika loose for both their sakes.

"Query—"

"No more queries, Savvy. Just file this under inscrutable human behavior and move on." Jorna would try to do the same.

"Acknowledged."

She reminded herself that Savvy had already improved drastically in the time they'd been working together, calibrating its approach and anticipating her needs to a startling degree. That more than made up for the queries that needed concrete answers to explain ineffable human behavior or hewed too closely to Jorna's personal life. Usually.

But she was feeling a bit prickly today. *Jumpy*, Meigs voiced in her head.

She headed to her quarters next door. She could have opted to stay in the residential sector with the rest of the staff, but that part of the Climasphere was still being built out when she'd been awarded her position, and she saw no need to change that now, given her workload. It was simply too convenient to have her apartment so close at hand.

The government-issued furnishings and hotel wall art weren't glamorous, but they provided a nice change of scenery when she was sick of data readouts and the hum of the gene sequencer in her lab. It was even marginally cleaner in here, though she supposed she could allocate a bit more time into her schedule to straighten up the place. Maybe she could deputize Savvy to help her get caught up with laundry if it was serious about supporting her well-being in all facets of her life, not just work-related ones.

She quickly showered and dressed for dinner with the commander. The tunic, slacks, and boots were well-worn but presentable. After being cooped up in the biosuit all day, she couldn't bear the thought of wearing anything more restricting than that. She pushed her still-wet, chin-length black hair behind her ears and returned to the lab.

Jorna sifted through a stack of papers and frowned. "Have you seen my touchscreen? The primary one, not one of the satellites."

Her voice pulled Savvy out of standby mode. "No. Perhaps it is still in your quarters?"

Jorna shook her head. "I didn't see it in there. I could have sworn I left it here before we headed out this morning."

"I do not detect its signal in the vicinity, Dr. Benton."

Which meant it either wasn't here or was but lost its charge. She sighed. "What else could go wrong today?" Savvy's eyes lit up. "No, don't answer that. It'll turn up eventually, I'm sure." She was out of time anyway.

"Did you want me to come with you to your appointments, Dr. Benton?" Savvy asked from the charging station.

Could it sense her reluctance too? Jorna started to shake her head, then stopped. "Actually, that's a good idea. If I tap my knee three times, I want you to announce that Meigs requires me to return to the habitat."

Savvy cocked its head in a crude approximation of curiosity. "You want me to lie to the commander?"

"I want you to make up an excuse to leave dinner early if I ask you to. So if it comes to it, yes."

It went quiet for a long moment. "Acknowledged," it finally said. "Query—"

"I am *not* explaining this to you, Savvy." And yet Jorna still felt guilty for keeping her assistant in the dark. She pinched the bridge of her nose. "Pay attention, and we can do the debrief when we get back, all right?" That was the best she could offer.

It blinked slowly. "So noted, Dr. Benton."

3

JORNA JAMMED HER index finger into the shuttle call button while Savvy idled beside her on the platform. She hadn't left her sector of the Climasphere in weeks. So focused on the harvest, she would oscillate between her lab, her quarters, the habitat, with occasional forays to the Tree Farm and Seed Bank to ensure a smooth transition into planting once the last transport was on its way. It felt strange to be going anywhere else.

It didn't help she was all up in her head thanks to Meigs, which never helped matters, calling into question her ability to navigate her meeting with Commander Kaysar with any sort of finesse. With the way Jorna was feeling now, outlook not so good.

Forcing those thoughts aside, Jorna frowned down at her boots. Leaks and fault tolerances were a slightly more palatable subject. Only a few meters of carbon nanotubes, steel girders, reclaimed polystyrene, and industrial air bladders separated her from the depths of the ocean.

That had been her only hesitation when applying for the position. She still had nightmares, where the waves could reach her childhood bedroom all the way in landlocked Colorado, after witnessing a significant stretch of Oregon coastline fall into the sea on the news when she was young. Much too young to understand what she was witnessing, only that it was awful. Unstoppable. Unexpected, yet obvious in hindsight.

Like so much else.

Even now, it felt like the whole platform swayed as the shuttle arrived, like her bed did whenever she was trapped in one of those dreams as the sea rose inexorably around her. Her imagination working overtime.

She felt better once they were on their way. Powerful magnets pushed the shuttle along the twenty miles of track that ran the entire circumference of the habitat, connecting dozens of work areas, holds, laboratories, and research clusters associated with the Climate Action Council as well as ones leased out to research institutions around the world. In moments, she and Savvy passed Engineering, numerous cargo holds, and the Aquaculture Research Institute.

With most of Jorna's horticulture techs on leave, these coming months were supposedly her downtime, where she could rely on the automated drone monitoring system for the habitat and focus on her own research, but she and Meigs were still putting out fires. She hoped the next round would remove the rest of the kinks in the process so she'd have the time she was promised. The dedicated time she'd worked so hard for, her reward for all the long hours and the sacrifices she made to get here for a cause she wholeheartedly believed in.

Not too shabby, considering where she'd started from. But that didn't mean she could take it easy.

"You have arrived at the medical sector," the intercom announced.

Jorna and Savvy disembarked. She instructed Savvy to wait for her in the sitting room and announced herself at the front desk. She was escorted past a quiet triage area to one of the patient rooms.

Dr. Rafa, a Black man with graying temples and a sharp-looking goatee, breezed in, touchscreen in hand, a med tech on his heels wheeling in a metal cart full of fluids and infusions. "Do you mind if one of our trainees shadows me today, Dr. Benton?" Rafa asked.

"Not at all." She knew firsthand how hard it was to maintain a large staff. She took off her tunic while the tech readied the IV.

Rafa scrolled through her medical record. "It's about time we saw you again."

"I know, I know. It's been busy, with the harvest and all."

"Well, I suppose I can't complain too much. Your colleague Meigs is even harder to pin down."

"Yeah, she's—*ouch*."

The med tech jabbed the needle into Jorna's arm and rotated it back and forth, looking for a vein. Fire blazed down Jorna's forearm, and she jerked away. The needle clattered to the floor. She hissed through her teeth as Rafa stepped forward and took over, his sure hands making quick work of the port. He glared over his shoulder at the cowering tech who swiftly made his apologies, grabbed the needle, and scurried out, the cart rattling as he went.

Rafa sighed. "Sorry about that."

"It's fine. Let's just say it's in keeping with the theme for the day I'm having."

"Well, we'll see if we can make it up to you during your session. Any changes to your health you'd like to discuss?"

Jorna shook her head.

"Headaches, sinus pressure, intrusive thoughts?"

She smiled nervously. "That last one's a joke, right?"

Rafa's expression didn't change. If anything, he seemed disappointed.

"Ah, nope," Jorna hastily said. "Nada." She should know by now not to underestimate her ability to make things awkward, no matter the situation.

Rafa looked down at his touchscreen one last time and nodded. "Well, that's it for me." He opened the casket-like gene therapy capsule, revealing the light panels that wrapped around the interior and the clear plastic table Jorna would be lying on momentarily. "Hop on in."

He secured her peripheral IV and handed her a pair of eyeshades. "Sweet dreams."

The capsule closed around her. As light bathed her body, her system was flooded with recombinant proteins, modified RNA strands, and nanobots. Even in a controlled environment like the Climasphere, she couldn't escape all the cellular damage she'd accrued from living on a badly damaged Earth for three decades. Growing up, Jorna's parents didn't allow her or her siblings to get the treatment, fearing it was a scam or a deep state conspiracy to control the population. But after her first round at a college clinic as an undergrad, she could feel the changes at work from the inside out. Less inflammation, more energy, better... *everything.* She vowed never to be without again. Or at least as much as her schedule allowed these days.

A soft chime woke her at the end of the procedure an hour later. For a long moment, she simply lay there in the darkness, still groggy but relaxed, like she'd had the best sleep of her life with none of the sleep debt she usually incurred from anxiety dreams and churning thoughts about her research. Even knowing she'd be seeing Commander Kaysar again didn't generate the customary panic. She was still on capsule time.

"Doctor, sorry to interrupt, but we need to get the room prepped for our next appointment," Rafa said over the intercom. Jorna nearly groaned as the capsule swung open. She managed to get the important parts covered just in time for him to bustle in, remove the line, and dab the site with some wound-heal. "You're all set. I've already put you down for the same time next week."

Still slightly buzzed from the procedure, she dressed and collected Savvy before making her way to the shuttle platform. She still had a few minutes before—

She came to a clumsy stop at the familiar face before her. The commander was already waiting for them? Jorna blinked back disbelief. Kaysar really wasn't leaving anything to chance.

One shoulder was resting against a support pillar in a deceptively casual pose, her dark brown hair swept back in a low bun. She was in her early forties but wore it well, her service uniform trim though she'd undone the top two buttons, baring the long line of her bronze throat. The result of a long day, or perhaps she had no concern over decorum now that she was officially off duty.

Jorna swallowed hard. Showtime. "Commander Kaysar, I didn't mean to keep you waiting."

She smiled, transforming her face from striking to startlingly beautiful. In Jorna's eyes at least. "Not at all, Doctor. I based my arrival on your appointment, and here we are." Kaysar's gaze traveled over to Savvy, her blue eyes alight with amusement and curiosity both. "I didn't realize you would be bringing your hardware along tonight."

"Savvy's been working through some theorems for me, and I wanted it on hand if the results come in," Jorna said quickly. Too quickly.

The commander arched a brow. "Ah. Well." She turned about sharply and gestured to the arriving shuttle. "Anything you'd like to see to before we head to my cabin?"

"No." The sooner they could get through dinner, the better as far as Jorna was concerned. "But we would be grateful for any engineering techs you can spare to help Meigs repair the horticulture drones that burned out during the harvest."

Kaysar nodded as they entered the shuttle. "Done."

"Thank you for your assistance in this matter."

"There's no need to be so formal, Doctor. We're happy to help however we can."

They arrived at the residential sector in under a minute, but it still felt painfully long as Jorna tried to interpret the commander's seemingly contented silence as they were whisked along the track. On the lower level, the clamor of the mess hall and adjoining common area carried to the upper floor where crew quarters fanned out in either direction. The commander waved them on down the right corridor, the metal planking ringing with their footsteps. "It's a bit busier around here since your last visit, Doctor. A new batch of trainees arrived from the mainland."

"If now's not a good time—"

"Nonsense. My work around here doesn't change, no matter how many of my crew members are about." She turned back to her. "I imagine that's the same for you."

"Yes, but I am grateful not to have so many people underfoot for a change now that the harvest is behind us."

"You speak of solitude, and here I am ruining it." Kaysar said it almost playfully, as if daring Jorna to contradict her. Assure her she wasn't ruining anything. A trap Jorna made no attempt to fall into. "Here we are."

Kaysar's cabin was located right before the corridor transitioned into conference areas for the senior crew, with the Bridge just past that. Jorna had been here once before for a dinner party with the senior officers, and she was missing their presence keenly as she followed the commander into a small but comfortable living area. Kaysar's bedroom was off beyond a door on the left side, and an archway on the right opened onto a small kitchen and dining area. Dramatic landscapes adorned the walls of the living room and abstract, model-sized sculptures in metal and ceramic were perched on mirrored shelves. The different artwork didn't feel pretentious but worked together to create a cozy sort of harmony.

Commander Kaysar's cabin was a home she took with her. Jorna's was merely a place to live and nothing more. That hadn't bothered her until this moment. As she sat down in one of the overstuffed chairs, it felt almost as if the commander had draped a warm arm over her shoulders in welcome.

Savvy trailed in after them and gave Jorna an exaggerated wink before standing stationary by her side. They would have to work on that later.

The commander returned from the kitchen with two glasses of red wine. She handed one to Jorna and clinked them both together.

"What are we toasting?" Jorna was almost afraid to ask as the commander took the opposite seat.

"Well, being in person for one. This is much more pleasant than commlines or viewscreens."

Kaysar didn't add, "Don't you think?" for which Jorna was eternally grateful. She wouldn't be able to answer truthfully without encouraging whatever this was between them. Nothing—it was nothing, she reminded herself.

"But," the commander continued, "the timing just felt right."

Kaysar gave her a brilliant smile, and Jorna looked away, uncomfortable with the corresponding jolt to her stomach. How could she have thought to keep Commander Kaysar running in the background of her life so long without making an attempt to address things? And now, here she was, chewing up all available memory. Jorna could barely remember herself when the commander looked at her. "Felt right?" Jorna repeated unsteadily.

"Surely you have moments of intuition that guide you in your work, same as mine. Or is it all data-driven questions, answers, and probabilities?"

Jorna shook her head. "I usually leave the probabilities to Savvy."

The commander chuckled like Jorna knew she would.

"My scientific training does affect how I approach things, it's true," Jorna continued, "but to say I don't follow my gut is also incorrect. My gut is what helps me to decide what methods to employ, where my interests lie, when to keep at something…"

"And when to quit?"

"Yes, exactly." Pleased she managed some reasonable small talk under the circumstances, she took a sip of wine. She could tell it was very good, even though she could also tell her palate wasn't sophisticated enough to catch all the nuances. "I imagine your gut is what also makes you such a good leader."

Commander Kaysar went still as if suddenly uncertain. "Is that a compliment, Doctor?"

"Merely an observation. One does not get to where you are without good instincts."

She tapped her fingers idly on the side of her glass. "I suppose it's true. I have a knack for reading people, and that's served me well over the course of my career." She leaned forward, her blue eyes twinkling. "Would you like a demonstration?"

Jorna blinked, unsure how to answer.

"Let's take you. Dr. Jorna Benton. Thirty-eight years old with advanced degrees in botany and biochemistry, commendations from the Academy of the Sciences, considered to be an expert in plant pathology and genetics, and no complaints from any of your colleagues or crew."

"Yet."

"Yet," Kaysar readily agreed. "But I'm still looking for the version of you from when we first met. Where is *she*?"

The servos responsible for Savvy's head tilt were painfully audible in the silence that fell as it looked from the commander to her. Jorna's mouth was suddenly drier than the air on the desert tier as she struggled to clear her throat. "I left her behind."

"Hmm." The commander gave Jorna a thoughtful look over her glass. She tried very hard not to react to the speculation in Kaysar's gaze. "As I'm sure you've already guessed, that's why I invited you here today. We're overdue to talk about what happened. Call me old-fashioned for wanting to do this in person, but with the harvest behind us, we have no more excuses."

The glass in Jorna's hand felt particularly delicate. She was a fool to come here, to think she could get through this unscathed. But she still had to get through the evening.

Knowing she was out of time, she leaned forward in her seat. "Had I known who you were that night, I wouldn't have let things go so far. It was a mistake, and I apologize for my unprofessional behavior. You have my assurance it won't happen again or affect our working relationship."

There. She sat back, took a breath. It was done.

"Oh, but I'm afraid it already has. Isn't that why you've been working so very hard to avoid me?"

Jorna set her glass down on the side table and rested her hands on her knees, acutely aware Savvy was watching on. "I have nothing but the utmost respect for your role on this mission."

The commander dismissed her words with a hand gesture. "I don't need your respect, Doctor. I have a whole crew full of people who are required to respect me."

Jorna tapped her knee once, twice, but she couldn't quite squelch her curiosity. "Then what is it that you do want from me, Commander?"

"You run the habitat." Kaysar made a fist with her hand, mimicking the sphere. "I run the rest." She drew a circle with her index finger. "Everyone else is subordinate in some way." She held up her hand, palm out, and then let it fall to her lap with a delicate twist of her wrist.

Jorna's finger hovered over her knee for a long moment, then she placed her hand to the armrest of her chair, deliberately exaggerating the movement so Savvy couldn't possibly misinterpret it. "I see. But I think it's only fair to point out in a true emergency your authority outranks mine."

Kaysar's grin could cut glass. "That's true, but I hope you won't hold it against me." She pressed her lips together, as if mentally composing whatever she planned to say next. Jorna knew she should tap her knee once more and get the hell out of there, but her hands stayed wrapped around the armrests, braced for impact.

"My career has overshadowed or outright prevented the majority of my relationships over the years." Any good humor in the commander's voice had been replaced with solemn earnestness. "At the gala that night, you gave me a glimpse of what it was like for someone to see *me* without my career getting in the way or coloring their perception of me before we even got the chance to know one another." Kaysar's eyes sought out hers, defiant, hopeful, and so blue it was like looking into the sky on a rare clear day back home. "I just want you to know I would not be opposed to feeling that way again."

Kaysar looked away, breaking contact, and it was like Jorna was slowly coming back online after a hard reboot. The commander was still interested? After everything Jorna had done to pretend they were nothing to one another? She was dizzy at the thought she'd been invited here, not for the dressing down she feared, but for an opportunity to pick back up where they'd left off. An opportunity she didn't deserve.

"Anyway," Kaysar continued, "I know from experience seven years is a long time to go without someone in your life who you can relate to on an equal footing."

There were too many possibilities to parse in that statement, so Jorna stuck to facts. "And you think that's me?"

"Well, it's certainly not Dr. Rafa."

Jorna's mouth quirked at that. She was nearly certain Rafa wasn't interested in women, no matter how attractive they were, not that it was any of her business.

The commander shrugged. "I've come to realize you're someone who'd appreciate me laying out the facts, as it were, so here we are."

"I understand." And Jorna did, all of it. But this was a contingency she hadn't planned for. Hadn't dared to. "What you're asking is—"

An alert blared from the console. The commander held up her index finger as she opened the commline. Jorna pulled in an unsteady breath, unsure if she was relieved or frustrated at the interruption. She resisted the urge to look at Savvy and contemplated the patterned carpet as if it could solve all her problems. She'd settle for an answer to the one seated before her.

"Commander, the diagnostic of the navigation system you requested is now complete. No issues were detected. We should be able to get underway tomorrow as planned."

"Thank you. Kaysar, out." She returned her attention to Jorna. "Sorry about that."

Their previous conversation rushed back over her, unavoidable, unfinished. Whatever Jorna had envisioned for tonight, it wasn't this. She'd reasoned they were two working professionals, both of them motivated to put such an awkward occasion behind them and move on. Her brain protested at the "awkward" descriptor. Even now, her gaze kept darting to the commander's throat, the hint of collarbones beneath the uniform that Jorna already knew the shape of. But parts of the encounter had been awkward, particularly at the end, so it still counted. But what Kaysar was suggesting...

A chime from the kitchen derailed her thoughts. Commander Kaysar got to her feet. "Ah. That should be our dinner."

As Jorna stood to follow her into the kitchen, Savvy's eyes lit up to address her. "Would you like me to continue monitoring you for the agreed-upon signal?" It winked twice, its voice painfully loud.

"Just..." Jorna rubbed the back of her neck, stimulating her vagus nerve in the vain hope it would bring her some much-needed clarity. None was forthcoming. "Stand by."

Savvy turned so it was now oriented on the dining room. Jorna couldn't blame it—this evening was turning out to be far more interesting than monitoring respiration rates or tracking growth charts.

"Don't worry, bot friend," Commander Kaysar called out

as she set the table. "Dr. Benton's honor is safe with me."

Jorna shook her head. "That's not... It isn't..." Maybe she'd be able to laugh about this in the future, but being sucked into one of the tidal generators right about now would be preferable to this... farce. Not that she deserved anything else.

Commander Kaysar just laughed at the look on her face. "Come. Eat," she said not unkindly. "I promised you dinner, so dinner is what we'll have."

4

WHATEVER THE COMMANDER had selected from the printer *did* smell delicious.

With no little reluctance, Jorna joined her at the table. The food printer had somehow created chicken roulades stuffed with spinach and mushrooms and topped with a garlicky herb drizzle.

To ensure everyone's dietary needs were being met, food printers had become commonplace in the last few years to dress up macronutrients extracted from an exhausted food supply, easing the impact of food shortages, which had become a global game of Whac-A-Mole, and drawing down the need for animal protein to more sustainable levels. Once a week, the food hall would create a menu sourced from plants grown on board the sphere, but they were kept separate from *her* plants in the habitat. After all, Jorna wasn't in the business of food production—she was rebuilding entire ecosystems by growing as many viable specimens as she could and seeing them safely transplanted to their forever homes. She kept intending to sample one of the weekly non-printed meals, but it never seemed to work out with her demanding schedule. Plus her own food printer was *right there* in her apartment, the convenience outweighing novelty every time. But it had never created a meal quite like this.

Jorna picked up her fork and stared at it like she had to relearn etiquette all over again. The commander seemed content to simply eat, so Jorna did the same, each element utterly delicious. When she took another sip of her wine, she realized the flavor perfectly complemented the meal.

The commander watched Jorna as she swirled her last bite through what little sauce remained on her plate. At least her stomach was pleased with her decision to stay for dinner. "That was excellent. Your printer must be different than the one I have because it could never render all those distinct layers."

Kaysar grinned. "That's because I made the Gourmand Elite a condition of my acceptance of this position."

Jorna looked at her in surprise. "You can do that?"

Kaysar's smile softened with something close to but not quite like pity. "It's all about knowing your worth." She waved to her across the table. "You had to compete to get this assignment, yes?"

Jorna nodded. She, along with dozens of other early-career scientists supposedly full of potential brilliance, had all vied for a chance to lead one of the Climaspheres into history. "In addition to rigorous written and oral exams, they had us blindfolded and placed in different rooms that recreated each of the biomes to see if we could identify them."

"And how did our intrepid Dr. Benton do?"

A dull flush crawled up Jorna's neck. "I was the only candidate who correctly identified them all."

"I knew it," Kaysar said proudly.

Jorna shrugged, uncomfortable with the praise. "It more than made up for placing third in the physical fitness test." Some things couldn't be taught, and bone-deep recognition of one's environment was one of them. "In the end, it was clear they wanted someone young enough to make a multi-year commitment but with enough expertise to do the job." At times when she wasn't so overloaded with her responsibilities, she was still amazed she'd been the one selected for such an honor.

"Goldilocks."

Kaysar's remark threw Jorna only for a moment. "Yes. They needed someone not too old, not too inexperienced—"

"But just right." Kaysar gave her a soft smile. "When you won, I bet you were so grateful to have been chosen, details like what kind of food printer you got didn't matter."

Jorna conceded that with a tip of her head. "Or I didn't know to ask about them in the first place."

"Exactly. I, on the other hand, spent too many years eating out of subpar mess halls or choking down MREs. There are some things I'm no longer willing to compromise on—"

An alert chimed with another incoming message from the Bridge. "Commander, we just received a security briefing from the mainland."

"Thank you. Kaysar, out."

Her dining table doubled as a conference table with a holoprojector at the center. Her hands skated over the console, and in moments she pulled up a report on an attack on the Philadelphia shipyard, the same one the Climasphere mission had launched from six weeks ago. "They're saying it was a terrorist incident."

"Do they know who's taking responsibility for it?" Jorna asked.

"The God's Supplicants are suspected to be behind the attack."

Suddenly, the meal sat heavy in Jorna's stomach.

"You've heard of them?" Kaysar asked her.

Jorna wiped her mouth with a cloth napkin and folded it back up before placing it on the table. "Yes."

"From my time working with Earth Shield, I thought I knew all the active eco-terrorism groups."

"They wouldn't say they're terrorists, eco or otherwise, but they are a particularly zealous religious sect."

Kaysar frowned, her eyes slightly unfocused in thought. "Are they the ones who welcome the destruction of the world because it brings them that much closer to the Rapture?"

"Well, it's..." Jorna opened her mouth, closed it, then opened it again. She gave up trying to come up with a concise way to describe their accelerationist views and just said, "Essentially."

When she looked up, the commander was watching her again, her head cocked in curiosity. "That sounds like a story."

Jorna made a sound of protest in the back off her throat. "Growing up, some of my family members were involved in the church but..."

"Here you are."

Jorna nodded. She pressed down on the napkin seams, suddenly needing each crease to be crisp and neat.

"Family is complicated," Kaysar said, a momentary shadow crossing her face. "It must have been difficult to be true to yourself back then."

Jorna inhaled sharply. Sometimes it still was. "It was a long time ago."

"Well," Kaysar continued brightly, "it looks like you turned out just fine, Doctor."

"That's kind of you to say."

"None of that. Didn't I tell you? I'm an excellent judge of character."

No, she wasn't. Jorna wanted to tell her she was wrong about her. That what she wanted from her was impossible, no matter what she—

Her ears grew hot. It was time to go. Past time. So there was no time to return to their earlier conversation. She stood quickly, heedless of the way the commander's eyes widened in surprise. "Thank you for your hospitality, but I must be going." Jorna pointed Savvy to the door.

"Of course," Kaysar said smoothly. If she was disappointed, she didn't appear so as she preceded both Jorna and Savvy to the door and pressed the button to hold it open for them. "Perhaps," she said carefully, precisely, weighing each word, "we could continue these dinners if you're agreeable, Doctor. At the very least, you'll get to enjoy the Gourmand Elite, if not the company."

Jorna could say no and end this here and now. But she didn't want to disappoint the commander, not when she'd proven to be so understanding about everything. "That's very gracious of you, but I..."

"Dr. Benton's schedule is free most evenings," Savvy offered.

Jorna struggled not to throttle the automaton.

Commander Kaysar was grinning again. Jorna didn't think there were many things the woman wouldn't grin at. Kaysar's mouth firmed as if she had to forcibly repress her amusement and gave Jorna a formal nod. "That's good enough for tonight. Good night, Doctor."

"Commander."

The door closed, leaving Jorna in the hall with Savvy. Any lingering relaxation she felt from her time in the gene therapy chamber had been completely wrung out of her. "My calendar is my own to manage, Savvy." She could barely keep her voice civil given how keyed up she still was.

"Apologies, Dr. Benton, but you asked me to prompt you whenever you trail off mid-conversation."

It thought it was being helpful. That somehow made everything worse. "That was for times when we're discussing highly technical scientific phenomena. Not..." Whatever this was. "The situation with Commander Kaysar is very delicate."

"The commander is attracted to you."

Jorna glanced around the corridor, but it was thankfully empty. "Savvy," she growled.

"I observed her exhibiting all the markers for attraction. Increased respiration, heart rate, pupil contraction, vasodilation—"

"Doesn't matter. We are colleagues only." Jorna stalked down the hall as if she could outrun the conversation.

Savvy juddered along beside her as they made their way back to the shuttle. "Why? You are attracted to her as well."

"What? No. That's impossible."

"Your bio markers would indicate otherwise," it told her. As if she didn't already know.

Jorna grit her teeth. "What I *mean* is it's a complication neither of us can afford."

"Query—"

"No more. Not now," she said tersely. For all she knew, the commander could have accessed the security system and was listening in on their conversation at this very moment. No, Kaysar wouldn't do that, Jorna thought just as quickly, but it still didn't feel right talking about this while they were still on her turf. The rest of the walk and the shuttle ride passed in silence. It wasn't until they reached the lab that Jorna let Savvy speak again.

"Query. What made you decide not to use the signal to leave early?" The automaton seemed particularly animated this evening. Probably an emotional well-being subroutine or something that prompted Savvy's line of questions.

Jorna exhaled slowly. "Curiosity, I guess. The folly of human-kind."

"What did the commander mean when she asked about the version of you when you first met? I am not familiar with that expression."

Jorna pressed her lips together. "That's because it's not an expression. She meant that literally." Jorna sighed. She could feel the whole story, clamoring inside her, wanting to be told. "There was a gala on the mainland to celebrate the Climasphere's impending launch. I got there late thanks to…"

She winced at the memory. *Family is complicated*, Kaysar had said. Wasn't that the truth.

"It doesn't matter," Jorna continued. "What does is I was mad at myself for losing track of time, and I headed straight to the bar. I was besieged by donors and administrators almost immediately and just wanted to escape."

She'd been in no condition for the grip-and-grin bullshit, so she excused herself on pretense of finding the restroom. She ended up in the gardens at the back of the sprawling complex, prepared to tell anyone who called her out it was merely professional curiosity that had drawn her away from the festivities. And it had the benefit of being partially true—she'd been meaning to see them but never could find the time. Philadelphia had fared better than a lot of other urban centers along the East Coast when the seas rose, and the City of Brotherly Love was enjoying a new era of economic prosperity and growth as a result.

The gardens were comfortably dark, solar lanterns every twenty feet casting the boxwood topiaries along the perimeter in sharp relief. A small stream cutting through the flowering terraces swirled with bioluminescent algae. It was beautiful, the kind of place she wanted to get lost in, not beholden to anyone.

A place where she could be herself without the weight of responsibility and expectations crowding out all the rest.

"I ran into the commander, only I didn't know it was her at the time. We talked and—"

Jorna shook her head. She wasn't about to tell Savvy how reckless she'd been, but the memory of that moment was just as vivid as that night when Kaysar had stumbled upon her little corner of the garden. The darkness had hidden her from view until she nearly ended up in Jorna's lap.

She could still envision Kaysar's blue eyes, impossibly wide with concern, when she'd said, "Apologies. I didn't see you there. Are you hiding too?"

"Is it that obvious?" Jorna asked.

"Understandable, given the circumstances." She perched herself next to Jorna on the low wall separating the path from an arbor fragrant with night-blooming jasmine. "My cheeks hurt from smiling so much."

That had drawn Jorna's gaze to the woman's mouth, her lips full and soft as they curved into a pleased smile at Jorna's lingering attention.

Usually Jorna's interest wasn't so evident, preferring instead to move slowly, carefully, but something about the woman's poise, the way she leaned toward Jorna, her eyes twinkling with surprised interest, had made her careless. Or perhaps it was the rocks glass in her hand she'd been nursing.

Anything felt possible underneath a curtain of jasmine next to a beautiful woman.

She'd raised her empty glass in salute. "You don't have to smile anymore on my account."

Kaysar laughed. "Real smiles are no hardship. It's the fake ones that are so costly."

That night Kaysar had worn a slinky cocktail dress instead of her uniform. And with her hair down to her shoulders, Jorna could have been holding her ID badge in hand and still not known she'd been flirting with the commander.

"We walked right up to the line," Jorna told Savvy. And crossed several others, her still-fluttering heart reminded her.

She thought their instant attraction had been the alcohol. Or perhaps a desire to cut loose before the mission. Neither of them had brought up the impending launch, and there had been enough civilians at the gala—the engineers and techs who built it, project leads and staff members who kept the whole machine running—there was no reason to assume the woman would be on board the Climasphere the next day let alone be the one piloting the damn thing. More fool her.

"One of the administrators came upon us and told me who she was," Jorna continued, "which put a damper on things to say the least."

His smug words still rang in her ears. *I see you've already made the commander's acquaintance. Your obvious dedication to fostering good relations for the expedition is a model to us all, Dr. Benton.*

It was hard to be sure, given the turmoil she felt, but Jorna thought the commander had been just as surprised to find out who she was, since they had only interfaced through text-only means up until that point. But instead of Jorna's abject horror at hitting on a colleague, Kaysar had taken it in stride and was somehow still interested despite Jorna's efforts to pretend like it had never happened.

"The Climate Action Council has no stipulations on relationships between consenting adults so long as you are neither one's direct report," Savvy said, sounding like it was reciting the employee handbook.

"This isn't about rules and regs." How could Jorna explain whatever Commander Kaysar saw in her that night wasn't who she really was? The real her could only disappoint someone like Kaysar.

"You had already broken up with Danika, so you did not misrepresent your status to the commander."

So logical. Jorna wished it could be that simple. "It's not like I was looking for a relationship that night, Savvy."

"You wanted a distraction?" Savvy asked.

"I wasn't thinking about it in those terms." And it hadn't just been her ex she needed a distraction from. But that was as good an explanation as any.

"Based on my observations, Commander Kaysar is correct in her assertion you are uniquely suited to one another, given the constraints you are both operating under."

"And if it goes poorly, what then? We would still have to work with each other for *years*."

"You would do what you are doing currently by minimizing any nonessential reason for interacting with the commander."

Now Savvy was calling Jorna a coward. She must be a pathetic excuse for a human if even her AI assistant was commenting on it. "Commander Kaysar is a colleague and not someone I'd ever consider, if not for what happened. She's too…"

Jorna couldn't, wouldn't, put it into words. Not for Savvy. Not for herself. Better to just not go there at all. Her standard MO.

"You don't take it as a sign? You humans place so much stock in the workings of fate."

She snorted. "Maybe *some* humans, but not this one. I'm a scientist, Savvy. Chance and coincidences, yes. The hand of fate? No." She'd turned her back on that kind of nonsense a long time ago and wasn't about to change now. Not after everything she'd sacrificed to put as much distance as she could between herself and the Supplicants and anything else approaching organized religion.

"Query—"

She pinched the bridge of her nose. "No more, Savvy, please. I have a paper I need to send out first thing tomorrow." There was a call for electroculture impact studies that the editor had specifically asked Jorna to submit to, but instead of the honor it was, it felt like one more straw on her tired back.

"Acknowledged, Dr. Benton." Savvy duly went to its charging station in the laboratory while Jorna retreated to her quarters.

She went over to her desk and sank down in her chair, taking comfort in the familiar contours. But instead of working on her paper or getting some much-needed sleep, she searched the network for more information about the attack on the shipyard. She found a handful of articles describing how the unexpectedly sophisticated attack had shut down operations for the better part of a week. Her chest grew tight as she scanned the list of Supplicants responsible for the attack.

Breath gusted out of her, and she sagged back in her chair when she didn't recognize any of the names. Thank goodness. Until that moment she hadn't realized just how worried she was to find out if her parents or siblings had been associated with the attack.

She could rest easy on that front. They might be Supplicants—devout, unyielding, and completely intolerant of the life Jorna had made for herself outside the church—but they'd never condone an attack that could hurt any of

God's children.

Meigs messaged her, and she accessed the audio channel on her touchscreen. "Well? What did she say?" Meigs demanded.

Jorna struggled to shift gears. "What do you mean?"

"The engineering techs," Meigs said with no little exasperation.

"*Oh.*" Jorna had forgotten to follow up with the commander on that issue before leaving her quarters, but, "She said it was no problem." Which was true. Though Jorna wasn't exactly eager to engage with Kaysar again to confirm the arrangements. But that was a problem for the morning.

"Good," was the curt reply. "Meigs, out."

"Well, good night to you too," Jorna said to an empty line.

5

BY THE TIME Jorna returned to her laboratory the next day and thought to follow up with Commander Kaysar about the engineering techs, Savvy alerted her and Meigs there were six loaner techs incoming.

Jorna stared blankly at her work console as relief and disappointment warred inside her. She'd woken up to the same thoughts that had plagued a night of fitful sleep. Not planting schedules or results sets, not faulty drones or the abomination that was her lab. It was Commander Kaysar's face, looking at once hopeful and defiant.

I would not be opposed to feeling that way again.

If they hadn't been interrupted that night in the gardens, would they have spent the last six weeks dancing around one another? Or would they have found a way to muddle forward together?

Jorna groaned into her mug of chai tea. This was exactly

what she was afraid of—a Pandora's box of emotions overriding all her plans and responsibilities. But no matter what contingency she considered when it came to Commander Kaysar, Jorna simply couldn't afford the distraction. Not if she was going to make the most of her research hours.

That was the real reason she'd worked so hard to be selected for this mission: the dedicated time built into her position for research with unlimited use of the sphere's considerable computational power, generating and analyzing research data that would otherwise take her the rest of her career to pull together. No matter how she might wish she could give Commander Kaysar a different answer, she wouldn't risk her role on this mission. By the time it was over, she'd be able to harness all her findings and make her way to any research institute in the world. Maybe then she'd finally feel like she was a proper scientist and not the imposter she feared she was, no matter her degrees or her coveted role on the Climasphere.

Maybe she'd finally be able to put her family's past behind her then too.

It was no doubt the news of the terrorist attack that had brought all those old feelings of inadequacy to the surface today, but in truth they were always there, lurking about, even if she wasn't thinking about her family or the Suppliants directly. Better to stay busy so there was simply no time to dwell on that painful history. Luckily, she still had plenty of things to do.

Jorna resumed her rounds of the habitat, taking time to inspect the new planting sites established yesterday. Thankfully once her decisions were made, the drones could usually handle the rest. Her army of bots was the only way she could manage while the horticulture techs were away. And so far so good.

She directed the skiff along one of the irrigation channels that distributed desalinated water throughout the habitat to the tropical rainforest on Tier 2. The humidity plastered her hair to her forehead and fogged up her helmet despite the valiant efforts of her suit's built-in fan, but the plants were literally soaking it up and looking all the better for it. Savvy kept pace with her, carrying an assortment of testing equipment and supplies in its arms along with the emergency kit strapped to its back. They reached a row of jacaranda, already starting to bud despite being planted eight months ago. Jorna pushed off her helmet and breathed in the heavenly-scented purple flowers. If they smelled this good now, she could only imagine how much better they'd be when the Climasphere reached the coast of Argentina, where they'd eventually be harvested.

"Dr. Benton, has your helmet malfunctioned? Shall I implement emergency protocols?"

"I'm *fine*, Savvy," Jorna said, taking the opportunity to mop her face.

"This is a high voltage environment. The risk of shock—"

"Is theoretically possible, but not likely." Her non-conductive boots were the most important part of her biosuit, the rest arc-rated in case the electroculture gradient that ran throughout the tiers to accelerate growth ever discharged. "A few minutes of fresh air won't hurt." The weather was even cooperating for once.

"But—"

"We've been over this before, Savvy. One of the perks of dealing with plants is moments like this one. I'm not going to let overly strict safety protocols ruin it."

"Dr. Benton, my directives—"

"Savvy, I understand your concern, but I'm not taking an unreasonable risk here. Please accept that your charge will indulge in entirely too-human behaviors upon occasion, like this one. That way you can better calibrate your risk assessment going forward."

Savvy tilted its head. Jorna got the distinct impression it was disappointed in her. "So noted, Dr. Benton."

"Good. Now—"

The ground shifted under her feet. Awful groans echoed throughout the habitat as though the walls were grinding together. Then all was silent for a moment before alarms blared from a control panel embedded in the wall of the next tier.

"Savvy, get Meigs on the line."

"Incoming message from Commander Kaysar."

That would work too. "Let it through."

Savvy's eyes flashed, and Commander Kaysar's voice sounded loud and clear. "Dr. Benton, we have a problem."

"So I noticed."

"We were just about to make way to our next anchor point, but the sphere seems to be listing slightly at two o'clock, creating uneven draw on the engines. Any idea why?"

"Offhand? No. But Meigs and I will do some checking. Stand by."

Jorna signaled Savvy to switch the channel over to Meigs. "What the hell was that?" the chief engineer demanded.

"My guess is shear stress on the sphere when the engines engaged. The commander wants answers."

"Let's meet in the Overlook."

"Roger that. Benton, out." Jorna turned to Savvy. "Come on."

They hurried back to the skiff and returned to the hangar. Jorna traded her biosuit for a rumpled lab coat before they headed to the elevator that climbed one of the curved support columns all the way to the top of the dome. The ride was smooth enough you could almost forget the carriage was essentially hanging over the habitat like an inverted roller coaster car being towed to the highest point of the track. Thank goodness the engineers had opted not to include windows into the lift design. The view from the Overlook was overwhelming enough since it was essentially a panopticon, giving them nearly 360-degree views of the different tiers spiraling down the sides toward the sea.

Glittery gold afternoon light shimmered through the habitat. She was far enough away from the water, it elicited only a distant pang of unease. But the view still made Jorna dizzy. Not only because of the perspective—though that definitely was a factor—but also just seeing the magnitude of what the sphere contained, the different environments the plants were intended for all together, the generations of humans they'd support, and even more knock-on effects she couldn't possibly predict. All of it rippling out from their work on the Climasphere. Such things could be counted and quantified, but only up to a point. Beyond that, Jorna could only marvel all over again that she, once upon a time a kid from rural Colorado, had been chosen for this mission.

She wouldn't see that trust misplaced.

She forced herself to look away and started scrolling through the camera feeds throughout the habitat to see if anything had been damaged. Luckily the tiers, ranging from the coastal flats of Tier 1 to the alpine tundra of Tier 9, seemed to be unaffected.

Meigs thankfully wasn't too far behind. She bustled in, smelling of the machine oil that stained the front of her coveralls. "Sorry. I was in the middle of drone surgery."

"No problem. Visual inspection of the habitat has revealed nothing so far." Jorna gestured to the control panel. "Any idea what's going on?"

Meigs shook her head as she stood at the workstation next to Jorna's, looking down at the display. "We'll just have to check everything."

The last time the two of them had been up here together was when they were running their last-minute checks before the launch. And there had been no problems regardless of whether the Climasphere was en route somewhere or safely anchored until now.

"Everything checks out. Everything," Meigs said.

"But there's got to be something to account for why the sphere's listing." Jorna peered down at the habitat to get a better look at the two o'clock sector, which corresponded to Quadrant 3 of the habitat. Then across the sea to Quadrant 1 on the opposite side of the habitat. Tiers 3, 4, and 5 in that area had been nearly emptied of all biomass during the harvest. She double-checked the data feed sent over from the Bridge. "What if the two o'clock sector didn't get heavier, but the opposite side got lighter?"

A moment later Meigs swore. "That's it. The buoyancy

levels are off by a couple decimal places. Just under the amount that would trigger a warning."

"That should be impossible. Nothing's changed since we got underway. Nothing's changed..." Jorna's eyes widened. "*Except* for the tiers that were harvested." All the plants they delivered to South Carolina came from the wetlands biome on Tier 3, the grass and shrublands region on Tier 4, and the temperate forest plots throughout of Tier 5.

Meigs snapped her fingers. "Right." She pulled up the logs and started scrolling back through the timestamps. "The change doesn't show up until the week of the harvest."

A number of growing plots had been removed wholesale and transported to the mainland for planting. Others cherry-picked for particular specimens. "That must be what changed the distribution of mass even though we've already started planting the replacements." In fact, a few thousand tons of topsoil was due to be delivered next week once they anchored off the coast of the Dominican Republic.

Meigs squinted down at the different biomes spread out in concentric rings below them. "I can redo the calculations, but we're just going to run into this issue again after the next harvest."

Jorna frowned. "Savvy and I will run an analysis to see what the optimal distribution of mass is for the tiers and make sure our replanting strategies match that going forward."

Meigs nodded. "You'll want to look at the tolerance testing the engineers did as well. See what assumptions they made for their calculations, because something sure as hell is off."

Jorna tipped her head to Savvy. "So noted," it responded.

She blew out a breath she didn't realize she'd been holding. "And I'll report in to Commander Kaysar." She'd promised the commander *and* herself she wouldn't let what happened affect their working relationship. Though it did feel like the universe was keen to test that resolve.

As they took the lift back down to the science corridor, Jorna gestured to Meigs's grease-stained coveralls. "Dare I ask how things are going with the drones?"

Meigs groaned. "Those new techs know how to handle cleaning bots, but not horticulture drones. But they're learning."

"That seems like a step in the right direction."

"Yeah, well, I just assumed they didn't know what they were doing because they kept asking me questions about every little thing, but it turns out I was wrong about the rotors. That one pollinator drone is still hosed, but the issue only affects maybe fifteen in total."

"Then what's the issue?"

"We found a lot of fiddly problems with *all* the drones we examined. Missing screws, network pairing issues, sensitivity thresholds needing instrumentation calibration. Really shoddy work."

Jorna crossed her arms. "Sounds like one of the horticulture techs didn't know what they were doing."

"Or didn't care."

Just what they needed. "I thought we screened for these kinds of sloppy mistakes."

"We did. I've been too busy babysitting the new techs to check the maintenance logs, but that's my next step."

"If it's an isolated tech who got in over their head, that's one thing," Jorna said. "If it's more widespread, I guess we'll have to revisit our processes for drone maintenance."

Meigs groaned. "Why not? We're already overhauling everything else so the next harvest won't be such a trash fire."

"It wasn't *that* bad considering it was our first one. Plus we learned so much." All the training in the world couldn't compare to the hands-on, hard-won experience of the inaugural harvest.

"Yeah, well, ask me that some other time when I'm not cleaning up someone else's mess." Cranky was Meigs's default setting, so Jorna tried not to take Meigs's frustrations personally as she peeled off for Engineering.

Savvy asked, "Did you want me to accompany you to the Bridge?"

Jorna held back a sigh. "Not this time. I want you focused on this new issue with the habitat, and I'll check in with you when I get back."

"Understood."

Jorna took a shuttle directly to the executive sector. Using her reflection in the shuttle windows as a guide, she hastily pushed her helmet hair behind her ears. Her grimace flashed across the glass. She didn't care how she looked when working with Savvy or Meigs or any of her horticulture techs. But Commander Kaysar was different— of course she was—on every possible metric. Only Jorna's best would do.

Her credentials admitted her onto the Bridge. Commander Kaysar was at one of the four workstations that flanked the commander's post in the center of the room with her second, Lieutenant Goh, in deep conversation.

"Dr. Benton on the Bridge," the officer at the comms station announced.

The commander turned to greet her. "Doctor, thank you for joining us." She held up a finger, finished her conversation with Goh, then gave Jorna her full attention. "Sorry about that. You caught us right at shift change. You have an update on the habitat?"

"Yes. We were able to determine the distribution of mass on the sphere had changed after the harvest. We believe that's responsible for the listing. Meigs is currently making the adjustments to the ballast tanks, and we should be able to get underway once that's complete. I have Savvy crunching the numbers to find the ideal distribution of mass across the tiers so we won't have to worry about something like this happening again."

"Excellent. I look forward to your report." She nodded to Goh. "The Bridge is yours. Doctor, walk with me. I have a couple more questions." Jorna followed the commander into the hall. "I don't recall any warnings about the arrangement of plants on the tiers and their effect on the Climasphere," Kaysar said as they headed toward the shuttle platform.

Some of the tension knotting Jorna's shoulders loosened. "I'm glad to hear it because Meigs and I were just as surprised. But it makes sense that when some of the plots were removed during the harvest, it was enough to throw things off."

Commander Kaysar nodded. "I'm relieved that's all it was. After hearing about the attack on the shipyard, my thoughts first went to sabotage."

Jorna shoved her hands into the pockets of her lab coat.

"This was just an oversight on our part, I'm embarrassed to say."

"No need. I haven't heard of this issue affecting the other Climaspheres. We may have just been unlucky. How will you plan around this issue going forward?"

"Most likely we'll have to do more individual transplants for the next harvest, but at that point I should be able to plan things out to optimize yields. Kind of like three-dimensional fallow field rotations."

They came to a stop, and the commander turned toward her, watching her expectantly with an amused smile.

Jorna's face heated at the scrutiny. "What?"

"Nothing. It's just..." Kaysar pressed her lips together for a moment as if repressing a smile. "It sounds like we're in good hands. Was there anything else?"

Anything else? Jorna blinked. Now that she'd gotten the commander up to speed on the situation with the sphere, she should go on her way. Instead, she could only stand there as the significance of what had been said last night washed over her. She studied Kaysar for... Jorna didn't even know what she was looking for. She just wanted to look her fill in a way that had been impossible before now, when she thought Kaysar wanted to put the whole situation behind them.

The commander folded her hands in front of her as if girding herself to deliver unwelcome news. "I want to apologize for the position I put you in yesterday. I hoped... Well, what matters is—"

"No." Jorna pulled the word from somewhere deep inside. Last night, the commander had opened a door between them, but it was up to Jorna to walk through. She still wasn't certain she *could*, not without upending everything, but she wouldn't see Kaysar lessen herself because of Jorna's own shortcomings. "You have nothing to apologize for. I... After what happened, I didn't know how to approach you, and even if I did—"

Fear. Risk. And the awareness that still burned bright between them in the empty hall. Jorna wished for just once in her life what she wanted wouldn't threaten everything else she'd worked for.

She searched Kaysar's face as if what she should say was written on her skin. But Kaysar's eyes were the only answer Jorna could find, impossibly blue.

Impossible.

Kaysar reached out and tucked an unruly lock of hair behind Jorna's ear. She didn't dare breathe as Kaysar's hand drifted down and came to rest on Jorna's shoulder. "It's all right. You don't have to explain."

Jorna wanted to. The heat of Kaysar's fingers sank through the material of the lab coat and Jorna's shirt underneath, spreading to the skin below. Jorna took Kaysar's other hand in hers, lacing their fingers together. "Commander—"

"You don't have to call me that when we're like this, Jorna," Kaysar said softly.

Like *this*, when work was the last thing on Jorna's mind. "I—"

A distinct boom rattled the entire corridor. The floor lurched beneath their feet, lifting and resettling in the span of a second. Jorna staggered into the wall and braced herself against the metal paneling. Commander Kaysar fell to her knees as the corridor heaved about a few seconds more, then stilled.

"That wasn't the engines, was it, Doctor?"

As Jorna helped the commander to her feet, her stomach was somewhere in the vicinity of her ears. "I don't think so. That felt a hell of a lot closer."

6

COMMANDER KAYSAR DIDN'T look particularly rattled, just pissed off, as she stood tall. She was only an inch or so shorter than Jorna—her force of presence just made her seem taller most of the time.

"Are you all right?" Jorna asked.

"Just shaken up a bit. You?"

"Same," Jorna replied, doing her best to mean it.

Kaysar looked down at Jorna's hands, still gripping Kaysar's elbow and forearm as if the commander was in danger of falling again.

"Oh. Right." A flush crept up Jorna's neck as she belatedly let go.

Kaysar didn't say anything as they retraced their steps back to the Bridge, for which Jorna was eternally grateful. That, and not having Savvy along this time to witness her foolishness. She could only imagine how that would influence its psychological profile of her.

"Report," Commander Kaysar demanded as soon as the doors whooshed open to admit them.

"Commander on the Bridge," the comms officer announced.

Lieutenant Goh answered right away. "There's been an explosion near the science sector. I've issued an emergency shelter-in-place order and instructed the security team to investigate." He had the feeds from the security cameras on-screen, displaying the corridor where the explosion must have happened. Low-hanging smoke partially obscured metal and plastic shards streaking the floor like singed confetti. It was hard to be certain, but it looked like one of the research clusters the next shuttle stop down from Jorna's lab.

"Status of the hull?" Kaysar asked.

"Intact."

The icy tension in the commander's face thawed slightly as they watched the feed. "Run it back thirty seconds," she ordered.

Thankfully it was after-hours, and the hall appeared empty of any personnel. A series of laboratories lined one side of the corridor. Only emergency beacons illuminated their interiors. Definitely shut up tight for the evening. A flash of light emanated from the lab closest to the camera. The explosion filled the screen for maybe three seconds, then cleared slightly, revealing the carnage from the wall being blown to bits. Strong enough to rattle the sphere, but not enough to damage its integrity.

"Any transponder signals picked up?" Commander Kaysar asked.

"None that were unusual," Goh replied, which only deepened the commander's frown.

"We have an incoming report from the security team," the comms officer announced.

"Let it through."

Replacing the stream of the lead-up to the explosion, a female security officer spoke to a camera drone. "This is Carolina Alvaro, Security Team Leader."

"Damage?"

"Minimal, considering the jolt we just felt. We suspect the explosion originated from one of the wall panels. My team's assessing the rest of the science sector to see if there are any other locations that have been compromised."

"What research group uses that space?"

"The manifest says it's registered to one of the gene-splicing labs." Labs responsible for creating new plant strains and testing them to survive, no matter what they faced outside of the Climasphere: polluted groundwater, exhausted topsoil, irregular rainfall, blistering sun.

"Could anything they were working on be responsible for the explosion?" Kaysar asked.

Alvaro shook her head. "I'll know more once I have a chance to interview Dr. Charanda, head of the unit. I've sent one of my officers to collect her."

"I want your report sent to my account. Same with all associated data feeds."

"We'll see to it, Commander," Lieutenant Goh said.

"My team's collecting DNA evidence as we speak, and we'll be sending it on to the med lab for processing," the security officer went on. "Though there'll likely be multiple samples to sift through."

"Good." Commander Kaysar turned to Goh. "I want to be alerted as soon as those results come in."

"Understood."

Commander Kaysar faced Alvaro once more. "Anything else?"

"Not at this time. Once the security sweep's done, we'll lift the lockdown."

The security officer's feed terminated, and Jorna took a breath, trying to take in all that had happened, and so quickly.

Commander Kaysar tapped her chin with her fingertip. "We're extremely lucky this wasn't worse." She pitched her voice to address everyone on the Bridge. Jorna had no formal military training, but even she stood a bit straighter at her tone. "Getting to the bottom of what happened is our highest priority."

"Yes, Commander," Lieutenant Goh said with a crisp nod. "I'll take full responsibility for the investigation. And you can count on Alvaro. I trained her myself." He paused for a moment, then squared his shoulders as if steeling himself to say something unpleasant. "As you can see, everything that can be done is being done. I don't want your personal time taken up with this any more than necessary."

She snorted. "Is that your way of telling me to butt out, Lieutenant?"

A wry half smile flashed across his face. "Is it working?" Jorna got the impression this was a long-standing argument between them. "With the lockdown in place and the investigation going forward, there's nothing to do but wait. And in your case, rest since you've already put in a full shift today."

Commander Kaysar shook her head, a grin hinting about her mouth. "You want me to sit this out? Not on your life." With her relaxed posture and eyes that missed nothing, Kaysar seemed tailor-made for emergencies like this. Invigorated instead of anxious and ready for anything. "Now, I want us to reconstruct the timeline for that corridor for the last week. I want every person, bot, and drone accounted for."

As the crew got to work, Jorna slipped into the hall. She didn't want to stay on the Bridge and seem like she was hovering or second-guessing things outside her domain when Kaysar clearly had things under control. Besides, Jorna had her own responsibilities to see to, starting with making sure the habitat hadn't been affected by the explosion. She entered the small officer's lounge across the hall and messaged Savvy with her wristcom. "How are things over there?"

"No change, Dr. Benton, but I take it you will remain in the executive sector for the duration of the lockdown?"

"Yeah. Unfortunately, I'll be stuck here a bit longer. Let me know if anything comes up, all right?"

"Understood, Dr. Benton."

Jorna set up shop at one of the workstations and started chipping away at tasks that didn't require her to be in her lab or the habitat to execute. As the lockdown dragged on from one hour into two, she had to admit it was nice to have someone else in charge during a crisis for a change.

Commander Kaysar emerged from the Bridge sometime later, her gaze faraway, her face full of tension. Deep in thought as she walked past the lounge, and no wonder given what happened. When she saw Jorna, she stopped, eyes widening with surprise. "Dr. Benton, have you been out here this whole time?"

Jorna lifted a shoulder. "We're still locked down."

The commander shook her head. "And you've been left stranded over here as a result. I should have realized."

"I'm the last thing you should be worried about. Besides, it's not so bad." As if on cue, Jorna's stomach rumbled, and she winced. In all the excitement, she hadn't noticed how late it had gotten.

Kaysar chuckled. "Guess you've had a long day as well. Come on." She waved Jorna toward the hall, then turned when she realized Jorna wasn't following. "Let me feed you, Dr. Benton. To make up for the delay."

"That isn't necessary." Nor was it a good idea after what had almost happened between them earlier. What part of Jorna still wanted to happen.

"Nonsense. In fact, you'll be doing me a favor by giving me something else to focus on besides the investigation."

"You mean Lieutenant Goh will owe me one for not letting you get in his way?"

"Precisely."

"You're certain it won't be an imposition?"

"Not at all," Kaysar assured her.

Everything about the situation felt inevitable, inescapable. Jorna wasn't sure she even wanted to escape, despite knowing the risks of getting this—whatever this was—wrong. But she also knew she didn't want them walking on eggshells around each other for the rest of the mission. So when Kaysar gestured once more to the hallway, this time Jorna followed.

Kaysar's quarters appeared much like they had last

night, but less pristine, more lived-in, with an empty mug and a stack of data readers scattered across the coffee table. "Sorry about the mess."

She hurried over to the table to tidy up, but Jorna stopped her with a hand on her elbow. "No need to make a fuss. You didn't know you'd be entertaining tonight."

Kaysar cast a critical look over the room, and Jorna realized the woman was embarrassed. Until that moment, Jorna hadn't believed anything could embarrass Commander Kaysar, but it was clear she wanted things to be perfect for this impromptu visit.

"You should see my lab. Then you'd know you have nothing to worry about," Jorna told her.

Kaysar took a deep breath as if deciding then and there to stop agonizing over the clutter. "Is that an invitation, Doctor?"

Jorna's breath caught. Another door. Another opportunity to walk through. "We have a lockdown to get through first."

Kaysar nodded, her eyes twinkling as if she'd known Jorna would demur. "That we do." She headed into the kitchen.

Jorna followed and leaned against the doorframe as the commander poured wine. "Before I forget"—*Again*, Jorna added mentally—"I wanted to thank you for supplying Meigs with some extra techs this week. She was so happy to have the extra hands." Even if they were left stranded in the habitat when the lockdown started.

The commander arched an eyebrow as she handed Jorna a wineglass. "Happy isn't exactly the first term that comes to mind when I'm thinking about Meigs."

"Then let's say not entirely miserable."

Commander Kaysar chuckled good-naturedly, which Jorna had come to expect at this point. "I meant what I said earlier, Jorna. I really do appreciate having you here to keep my mind off the investigation."

"You think it's sabotage?"

"We'll see what the report says, but I don't see how it can't be. And I can't do anything about it until we have a better idea of what we're dealing with." Kaysar exhaled and rolled her shoulders. "I know you'd rather be anywhere else than here, but thank you for coming."

"That's not true," Jorna said unsteadily. "It's just I didn't plan for this—any of this—to happen. It makes things… difficult."

"Difficulty is irrelevant when the course is correct." Spoken like a true commander. Kaysar abruptly turned to face the Gourmand Elite and started fiddling with the controls. "What are you in the mood for?" she asked over her shoulder.

"It could be week-old leftovers, and it would still taste better than the vast majority of recipes my printer makes."

"No opinion? Really?"

"I trust you," Jorna said. "Your palate, I mean."

"I *see*." Jorna could hear the grin in Kaysar's voice even if she still had her back to her. "Well then, it's going to be a surprise."

Even now, the smells emanating from the prep area were mouthwatering while their meal was constructed out of protein peptides, carbohydrate ribbons, extruded lipids, and a dizzying array of flavor compounds. Jorna tapped her glass idly with her finger, trying to come up with just the right thing to say to keep things light and casual between them, determined to put aside any awkwardness.

They were both grown women. They'd find a way to muddle forward. *Together*, her brain unhelpfully added.

The commander beat her to it. "What were you working on when I found you?"

Jorna relaxed at the mundane question. "Oh, I was working on my report on the inaugural harvest." It was still early days, but initial feedback from their partners in South Carolina indicated there'd been very little transplant shock. Time would tell if the die-off stayed below her conservative estimates, but she couldn't help but be optimistic with how things were going so far. Every plant was a win, no matter how small. "But I have to admit the reporting requirements for the Climasphere are unlike any project I've been a part of."

Commander Kaysar nodded in sympathy. "We have a whole department over here responsible for documenting all the novel situations on board, on top of the expected ones. I guess that's the price we pay for being at the forefront of such an endeavor."

"True. Without Savvy's help incorporating all the horticulture teams' reports with the output from the automated monitoring system, I wouldn't have time for anything else."

"I'm glad to hear the AI assistant is working out. I always thought their wellness directives were a bit oppressive."

"That's one word for it." Jorna glanced about her quarters. "I see you don't use one."

"Not a physical one, no. But I do use a virtual assistant to help me document my work and all the little decisions I make around here. It also helps me keep track of every person, place, and thing on board the Climasphere."

"You mean you don't know everything? I'm shocked to hear it."

Kaysar leaned forward, blue eyes twinkling. "Well, now that you know my secret, I guess it's off to the brig for you."

Something warm and fluttery slid through Jorna as they looked at one another. "I'm beginning to think you never want me to leave the executive sector, lockdown or not."

The Gourmand Elite chimed, and Jorna blinked, momentarily thrown.

Not missing a beat, Commander Kaysar rose to her feet, drawing Jorna's gaze to the way her uniform subtly set off her curves. "It's all part of my master plan." With a grin, the commander waved Jorna toward the dining table. "Take a seat. I'll be right there."

Light and casual had veered pretty quickly into dangerous territory. Jorna clearly needed a new approach, but she found it nearly impossible to resist Kaysar's playful banter. Jorna resolved to talk about her latest research findings while they ate. How different electrical frequencies tailored to plants' unique circadian rhythms could stimulate growth. Which chemical formulations and watering schedules had the best yields on which varieties. Those fiddly details could pump the brakes on just about anything.

The commander was on her way back with their plates when the door to her quarters suddenly whooshed open. Her eyes widened at the interruption, and the color drained out of her face.

Alarmed by her reaction, Jorna whirled around in her chair. She was pretty sure an emergency override was the only way someone could get in here unannounced.

Lieutenant Goh stood in the doorway, armed with a stun stick, while two more security officers held microwave rifles at the ready.

Jorna gasped. Holy shit, was this some kind of mutiny? Then her brain kicked back on. The rifles were pointed, not at Commander Kaysar, but at *her*.

Their dinner plates clattered to the table, forgotten. "What is the meaning of this?" Kaysar demanded.

Goh gave her a barely perceptible nod, keeping his gaze locked on Jorna. "Apologies for the intrusion, Commander, but we have reason to believe Dr. Benton is responsible for the explosion."

Jorna's eyes widened. "Me? What are you talking about?"

She was hauled out of her chair, and a pair of magnetized handcuffs were slapped around her wrists. The commander watched on, her face cycling through shock and anger. But Jorna couldn't think of a single thing to say as she was marched out the door and taken to the brig.

7

THE CLIMASPHERE'S DESIGN had been heavily influenced by the military. It didn't matter that their primary mission was to cultivate and deliver plants. The sphere had the facilities to support a more *strategic* role in international relations if need be—cargo bays that could easily be converted to house troops, an offensive armament tied to the tactical workstation on the Bridge, and a brig that could accommodate a dozen detainees comfortably, far more if comfort was not a concern.

Jorna found herself introduced to the Climasphere's brig under much different circumstances than she'd ever imagined as she was brought to an interrogation room and cuffed to a chair by Lieutenant Goh. Another security officer took up position by the door.

Goh's near-constant scowl narrowed his brown eyes and pinched his mouth. They'd always had professional interactions prior to this, but now the head of security was overbearing, aggressive. And angry as he took Jorna's measure and began his line of questioning.

Not that Jorna had any answers, let alone ones Goh wanted to hear.

"Like I already told you. If I wasn't in the habitat, I was in the med suite or with the commander. Even if I wanted to blow up the sphere—which I emphatically don't—when would I even have had the chance to set all this up?"

"The security team determined an explosive device was hidden behind a wall panel in the science sector. How do you explain how your DNA was all over the panel in question?"

That didn't even compute. Jorna's brain was locked into fatal error mode as Goh watched on. "I can't," she said helplessly.

"Can't or won't?"

"I *can't*. I can't even imagine how it happened. I haven't been by that sector in weeks."

Goh grinned in a not-so-nice way. "Four days ago, we have you on camera walking down that corridor."

Jorna blinked. How was that even possible? "Four days ago? Yesterday was the first time I left the habitat since the harvest." And before that, just once to see Dr. Rafa for a full workup after the Climasphere reached its first anchorage point. "Ask Meigs or Savvy for access to the feeds there to confirm it."

"Feeds your clearance could easily alter if you so chose."

Jorna couldn't hold back an eyeroll. "Come on."

"No, you come on." Lieutenant Goh shook his head. "Something like this could have easily taken out the whole expedition."

"What possible motive could I have to destroy the sphere? It not only encapsulates my life in addition to all the others depending on this mission, but it literally represents the culmination of my entire career. You've got the wrong person."

"DNA doesn't lie. You should know that, Doc."

"It can be manipulated like anything else. And the longer you waste your time with me, the longer the real culprit has to get ahead of this investigation."

The door to the interrogation chamber flew open to admit the commander. Immediately, Goh stood taller and ceded the floor to her. Gone was Kaysar's earlier shock; when she looked at Jorna now, she was every inch the Navy captain she used to be. Jorna didn't know if she should feel relieved by that or not.

Kaysar's gaze swept over her, revealing nothing, before she turned to Goh. "Surely the handcuffs are no longer necessary, Lieutenant."

"She's still a terrorist suspect. We must take precautions."

"I've only seen circumstantial evidence of that so far."

"But—"

"Dr. Benton is not leaving this room without your or my say-so. In the meantime, we can afford to show her some courtesy, yes?"

With no little reluctance, Goh approached Jorna and removed the cuffs. He returned to Commander Kaysar's side and plunked the cuffs down on the table before them. Jorna jumped at the metallic clang—her nerves were wound tighter than one of the electrical coils powering the grid for the habitat.

"Now, Doctor, what can you tell us about God's Supplicants?"

A visceral jolt of revulsion darted through Jorna. "What? I *told* you. I left that part of my life behind a long time ago."

"First an attack on the shipyard we embarked from, and now an attack on the Climasphere itself." Kaysar kept her hands folded primly in front of her, her voice polite. *Distant*, Jorna couldn't help but notice.

"Are those the religious fanatics who think rehabilitating the Earth is some kind of sin?" Lieutenant Goh's gaze hardened when it returned to Jorna. "You're one of those cultists? She must have infiltrated the mission and sabotaged it from the inside."

"We don't know that, Lieutenant," Kaysar said sharply. "But I would like to understand that history better, considering the circumstances."

Jorna hated how easy it would be for them to use her past as a bludgeon and blame everything on her. She'd worked so hard, for so long, to escape that part of her life, and now it had stubbornly returned, refusing to stay buried.

The commander's gaze hadn't left Jorna's face. She merely arched her brows. "Well?"

"You must have some idea how much the success of this mission means to me personally. I would do nothing to jeopardize that." Jorna gave the commander a hard look. "Nothing." That was one of the reasons she'd worked so hard to keep Kaysar at arm's length as well. How could she not know that?

"It doesn't change the fact we have a middle-aged female that matches your description in the hallway that day," Goh cut in.

"Well, that could be dozens of people on board," Jorna replied.

Commander Kaysar sat down on the table opposite Jorna's chair. "Help me out here, Doctor."

"I don't know that I can. If I wasn't in the habitat, I was with you or Dr. Rafa." Suddenly she felt exhausted, her mind working overtime to explain the unexplainable.

Kaysar watched her a moment longer then turned to face the far wall. "Viewscreen on."

The raw feed from the hallway in question appeared, the time stamp four days ago.

"Commander, I must protest," Goh said harshly. "You're only giving our suspect an opportunity to pad out her story."

She ignored her security chief, keeping all her attention on Jorna as she watched the research corridor, full of crew-members going about their day. Then Jorna saw it: a woman slightly taller than average with a lean frame, pale skin, and chin-length dark hair striding down the hall. She kept her face slightly turned away as if she knew the camera was there. She wore a maintenance tech's jumpsuit.

Jorna wouldn't even know how to get one of those if she wanted to. She could only shake her head. "She does look a little bit like me but..." She exhaled shakily as the magnitude of the evidence came crashing down on her.

"Can you explain it?" Commander Kaysar asked in a hard voice.

Jorna shook her head back and forth and back again. "I can't. It's got to be a horrible coincidence."

Goh scoffed at that.

The commander just frowned. "Tell me about your

family, Jorna."

Her chest pulled tight as the knee-jerk instinct to avoid the subject swamped her. That was the *last* thing she wanted the commander to know about her.

"Humor me, please?"

Jorna sighed. "I already told you, my family belongs to a God's Supplicants sect, but I got out years ago." The commander merely looked at her, waiting for her to continue, seemingly full of endless patience. She wasn't going to be put off. Jorna wanted to throw up her hands in frustration at having to dredge up all that old history, but she feared any move she made would set Goh off. "My father was the equivalent of a pastor and raised me and my brother and sister in their traditions."

"Which are?" Goh demanded.

Jorna bit her lip. Where to start? "I assume you're familiar with the Garden of Eden? God's Supplicants believe interfering with all the plants and animals on Earth is a grave sin. That by altering their genetic structures, we are rejecting God's gifts to humanity and, by extension, his plan for Earth."

"So they're accelerationists?" Kaysar asked.

"Only in the sense that we should not harness advances in technology to better our lives and the state of the world to stave off destruction. We should leave things as they are, and if that means whole species die out, so be it, because that must be part of God's plan."

"They would have us set aside all human progress?" Goh asked, flabbergasted.

"If we had, the end times would be that much nearer, and they'd all be closer to salvation." Jorna hunched her shoulders. "I'm not sure when exactly—it kind of creeps up on you—but at some point I started questioning the church's truths. The rest is history. Around the time the government was cracking down on religious school standards, my siblings and I were placed in public school for a year. But that was enough to"—Jorna pressed her lips together, struggling to find the right words—"open my eyes, you know? I ran away from home not long after, put myself though college, and here I am."

The resulting silence was unbearable. "You have to understand, what we're doing out here? They think we're playing God by rebuilding Eden, which flies in the face of everything the Supplicants believe." She forced back a grimace. "That was part of the appeal of this mission, to be honest."

"Playing God?" Goh asked.

"What? No. Dedicating my life to something the Supplicants couldn't touch."

"The perfect cover," Goh said dismissively.

Kaysar tapped her chin. "Or a setup. How old are your siblings?"

"My sister, Karin, is older than me by about a year. My brother, Eskil, is two years younger."

She gave Goh a look like, "*See?*" but Jorna feared that was only wishful thinking on her part. "Does your family have anything of yours that would have your DNA on it? Baby teeth, locks of hair?"

Jorna started to shake her head, then stopped. She didn't think her mother was the sentimental type to hold on to such things, especially once Jorna denounced their ways. She had reached out to her family after undergrad to see if she could talk to Karin or Eskil, help them get out if there was the slightest possibility they were open to it, but she soon realized that was a no-go. She still flinched at the thought of her mother on the front porch, blocking her entry and berating her with the Devil's tongue, the foul language so derided in others, throwing enough salt in her face it stung her eyes and burned her nostrils. "I doubt it, but one of the things they did was prick our fingers to consecrate things in our blood so we'd leave our mark on the mortal world."

Kaysar's nose curled up with disgust. It was just for a moment, but the corresponding shame crashed down on Jorna nonetheless. There had been so many rituals she'd participated in or been subjected to growing up that repulsed her now. They shouldn't define her—they *didn't*, she reminded herself—but the guilt by association had never left her, even if, intellectually, she knew she'd done nothing wrong.

"I told you I don't believe that stuff." Jorna raised her voice. Angry all over again as the past she kept trying to outrun clawed her back into its clutches.

Commander Kaysar didn't react to her tone, only lifted a brow. "But your siblings still do?"

"To my knowledge, the church still fills every aspect of their lives." Jorna's voice caught, and she looked at Kaysar in dismay. "You don't think..."

"I do," she said grimly. "I've only recently had to brush up on the subject, but I think one of your siblings may be on board somehow and wants to not only see this mission destroyed but your reputation, your legacy, as well. What better revenge on someone who rejected the church's teachings?"

A wave of horror washed over Jorna, leaving revulsion in its wake. She hadn't eaten since midday, and between her interrupted dinner and the interrogation, her churning stomach was completely empty of everything but a slurry of nerves. "They're here and trying to frame me?" Even as she spoke the words she had trouble wrapping her head around such a concept.

The commander's patient face looked back at her, unperturbed. "That's the way I see it, assuming you're as innocent as you say."

That it was still a question in the commander's mind bothered Jorna almost as much as the possibility of her family's involvement in the sabotage of the sphere. "Can I see that footage again?" she asked.

"Of course." Commander Kaysar queued the sequence back up from the beginning. As Jorna watched, she tried to fit her siblings' appearance over the figure on the screen. "It *could* be one of them. I don't know. Is there more?"

Kaysar shook her head. "Whoever did this wiped the footage of the actual installation of the bomb. A simple loop. Sloppy, but effective to throw us off long enough for them to move on to their next target."

"Which is?"

She deflated slightly. "I was *really* hoping you'd be able to tell us that."

██████

THEY LET JORNA cool her heels in the interrogation room for she didn't know how long. She kept trying to reposition her body in the lone metal chair, but any comfort eluded her. And why shouldn't it? If Eskil or even more unbelievably Karin had somehow infiltrated the Climasphere, that could potentially be catastrophic for all on board.

But if Jorna had any hope after speaking with Commander Kaysar, it had imploded by the time she and Lieutenant Goh returned, her wearing a stony expression, Goh looking like he'd just won the lottery.

"What's wrong?" Jorna asked. "Has something else happened?" Prisoners did not get the benefit of receiving sphere-wide announcements. All the uncertainty hollowed out her stomach.

"We've determined the detonation device was a touchscreen registered in your name," Goh said.

The blood drained from Jorna's head, making the room spin. It all made a terrible sort of sense. Her likeness, her DNA, and now her touchscreen, all tying her to the explosion. "I couldn't find it," she said slowly, as if this was all a dream. "For the last couple of days, I scoured my lab and my quarters, but it never turned up."

Even though it was the truth, it had no effect on the serious expression on Commander Kaysar's face. A nightmare come to life.

"How convenient," Goh said blandly.

"I have an alibi. Commander Kaysar and I—"

"You could have easily used a timer for the detonation," Goh said. "As to your relationship with the commander, who's to say this isn't all an elaborate attempt at misdirection to gain her sympathies?"

"It wasn't. It's *not*." Jorna tried to catch Kaysar's eye, but the commander's professional mask was firmly in place. "I wouldn't have even come to the Bridge today if it wasn't for—"

"You are the one who signed off on the harvest plans," Goh said. "You could have engineered this entire crisis."

That was wholly unfair. The Climasphere had been tested and retested to ensure they understood what the maximum weight tolerances were, but how that weight was distributed throughout the habitat was apparently a lot more important than any of them had realized. "I did no such thing," Jorna said through clenched teeth.

Goh still had that smug look on his face. Kaysar stood there so precisely, so stoically, it was as if she was focusing all her energy on not reacting.

"I'm telling the truth, I swear it."

Goh's shark smile widened. "Then why did you leave out the part, *Doctor*, where you met with your sister in the lead-up to the launch?"

"Oh, that." Shit. Jorna's gaze darted to Commander Kaysar.

"That." The commander determinedly looked past her, keeping her voice infuriatingly neutral as she explained how routine surveillance of the Climasphere staff in the lead-up to the launch had captured Jorna's meeting with her sister. "It wasn't deemed noteworthy when it was initially processed, but clearly things have changed since then."

"That's a pretty staggering omission, considering everything that's happened," Goh said.

Jorna shook her head. "I hoped it wouldn't become relevant, believe me."

Commander Kaysar's blue eyes lanced into her. "I want

to believe that, Jorna, but you need to tell us what really happened that day right now."

Jorna didn't want to do this with Goh watching on, but she had no other choice. "You remember the night we met?"

Kaysar's mouth parted wordlessly, then she seemed to give herself a mental shake and waved at Jorna to get on with it.

"Well, earlier that day, my sister, Karin, approached me. I was cleaning out my office at the training center. I almost didn't recognize her, it had been so long. I admit I was touched she'd been so willing to see me face-to-face before we disembarked. I hoped she'd gotten out, you know? We walked to a café and talked. Little things at first, then she launched into her concerns for my soul. How there was no coming back for me, spiritually speaking, from this mission. How she'd never forgive herself if she didn't try to save me from contributing to so many of God's Children desecrating the paradise that is Earth."

Jorna noticed the confusion on Goh's face. "The Supplicants believe by restoring Earth, we are not only rejecting God's plan for us but also rejecting any possibility of salvation."

Commander Kaysar nodded to herself. "So all the people depending on the success of this mission—we're helping to lead all of them into sin as well?"

"*Unredeemable* sin."

Her frown deepened.

"When Karin realized she wouldn't sway me, things got ugly," Jorna continued. "She started screaming, saying I was the Devil, and I left. I was mad I'd wasted my time even giving her an opening." And it wasn't just anger. All the frustration and fear that had fueled Jorna leaving home in the first place came roaring back with an insistence she didn't know how to stop. "When I finally got to the gala, all I wanted was a drink—"

"And a distraction," Commander Kaysar finished for her. Something in her eyes dimmed. Something vital, and Jorna felt the loss like a punch in the gut.

"That's not—"

"I understand," Kaysar said crisply, as if deploying her ironclad professional demeanor could hide the flash of hurt Jorna had inadvertently inflicted upon her.

"Why didn't you report your contact with your sister immediately? If you had given security a heads-up, none of this would have happened." Goh had his arms crossed again. His disapproval might as well have been plastered on an LED billboard blaring behind him. "All employees must report any contact with suspicious individuals, including contractors like you."

"Karin's no terrorist." At least Jorna didn't think so. "Supplicants believe everyone in the community has a duty to ensure all members adhere to the tenets, and nowhere is this more important than in the family. She felt a personal responsibility to bring me back into the fold."

"Sure she did," Goh mocked.

"Enough," Kaysar said. "What's done is done. What I want to know is why you tried to hide it."

Jorna's temples throbbed, but the headache was nothing compared to how raw she felt divulging all these details she'd kept secret so long. "Because I was ashamed. Deeply ashamed of having ever been a part of that cult." And though it was true, she didn't feel any better for having said it.

"But you were so young," Commander Kaysar began.

"Guilt by association. I couldn't risk it. And I was afraid. I'd worked so hard to get to this point. If it came out I came from a family of Supplicants, would I still be here?" Jorna shook her head. "Li Ying would have taken my place in a heartbeat. If she knew about my past, she would have used it against me with the selection committee so *she'd* be the one in charge of the habitat, not me." She'd been the runner-up for the position. Brilliant, driven, and on standby to step in should Jorna be unable to participate for any reason.

Goh scoffed. "Well, it seems to me we'd be better off with Dr. Li if she had."

Jorna had no response to that. It was true. But did hiding her past make her an awful person? Surely everyone had something they secretly feared was holding them back, didn't they? Maybe not someone so starchy, like Goh.

Commander Kaysar gave her second an exasperated look. "That isn't helpful, Lieutenant."

"But her failure to take responsibility—"

"That's enough." Commander Kaysar pointed him to the door. "Leave us."

"But—"

"That's an order, Lieutenant."

Goh mashed his teeth together as he cast his furious gaze from Jorna to the ceiling, but whatever training or respect he had for Commander Kaysar won out. "Yes, Commander."

Kaysar held herself abnormally still until Goh left, the

door sliding shut behind him. Even then, she remained silent, staring at the floor.

Jorna willed her to look up. "You have to believe me."

When Kaysar finally faced her, she wasn't commander of the Climasphere, but a woman whose resolve had been deeply shaken. And it was all Jorna's fault.

"You have to understand, Commander, I never meant for any of this to happen."

She sighed. "Of course not. I know that. Deep down, Goh knows that. But what do we do about it? That's the question."

"At the gala that night—"

Kaysar's shoulders immediately stiffened. "We don't need to rehash the details, Doctor."

"We do. You have to understand the fundamentalism I grew up with didn't magically go away when I got out. It's like..." Jorna struggled to find the right explanation. "It's like a constant undertow swirling around my feet. Usually I can keep my balance, but sometimes it catches me by surprise and pulls me under. Living like that, always on high alert for someone to find out, helpless to counteract the inevitable judgment... It's held me back from a lot of things."

Emotionally closed off, driven to achieve what she could in a discipline that ran counter to every Supplicant tenet at the cost of everything else in her life.

Including the woman standing before her. Forget walking through the door. It had been slammed shut and locked up tight now that the truth was out.

"That night, reliving all the reasons why I left the Supplicants combined with anger at the family that disowned me, I was drowning. Then you came along like a breath of fresh air. I never wanted to let go of you. But when I realized who you were..."

"Yes, I remember that part quite well, I assure you."

Jorna's face grew hot with shame. "Don't you see? It was never *you* that was the problem. It was my behavior, threatening the job I wanted most in the world. The job that proved my past had no hold on me. And if I tried to explain that, it would lead us right back to everything I was trying to hide, and I couldn't let that happen."

The commander was quiet for a long moment, her blue gaze unreadable, then, "I understand."

Jorna wanted to believe that she did. Whether that would have any bearing on what came next, she didn't know. "Whatever surveillance you want to put me under, fine. But I've got to get back to the habitat. If we can't deliver the next round of plants—"

"I am very aware of our mission and all the ways in which it can fail, Doctor," Commander Kaysar replied sharply. "Technically, you're still a suspect. Until you're cleared, procedure dictates we must keep you detained." A frustrated sigh escaped her. "*But* while you're here, you can still confer with Meigs and your assistant if any issues arise during your absence."

Jorna relaxed at that. She could still do her work. That wasn't nothing. "Do you really think one of my siblings stowed away?"

Kaysar pinched the bridge of her nose. "It's too early to tell, but that's my operating theory."

"I swear to you, I never would have imagined they were capable of something like this."

"I believe you, Jorna." Kaysar smiled with a regretful sort of wistfulness. "But I am still responsible for the safety and security of the entire Climasphere. Until we know more..."

Jorna wasn't going anywhere. "I understand," she said slowly.

The optics weren't great to begin with, and if Jorna insisted on special treatment, it would only hurt both of their standings with the rest of the crew. Women in leadership positions had to play not only by the official rules but all the unspoken ones out there as well. Jorna wouldn't ask the commander to choose her over that.

But Jorna didn't know what to do about Kaysar's pensive demeanor as she gathered up the handcuffs. Like she was already lamenting the possibility of a relationship between them after all that had happened.

Jorna wasn't quite ready to give up. "When this is all over—"

"A lot of things have changed these last few hours. Neither one of us is in a position to make any promises," Kaysar said resolutely, as if she had to remind herself of that as well.

That was it, then. Jorna could only watch as Kaysar shrugged back into her cloak of professionalism and left the room to confer with Goh in the hallway. Jorna got to her feet, and simply stood there for a long moment. The panicky fear from before was gone, but she still felt drained by recent events. She stretched out her arms. It didn't help the knots in her stomach, but she didn't think anything would until they found whoever was behind this attack. Preferably the sooner, the better. Even if the culprit was a member of her own family.

She consulted her wristcom. "Savvy? It's me." She gave Savvy a highly abbreviated overview of what happened, grateful to have something else to focus on besides Kaysar's disappointment in her.

"That must explain why I have been fielding queries as to your whereabouts since this mission started. As well as a number of unauthorized attempts to access my data stores."

Jorna grimaced. She knew Lieutenant Goh wasn't about to give her the benefit of the doubt on anything at this point. "Security is just being"—she glanced around the room, certain there had to be cameras somewhere even if she couldn't spot them—"thorough."

"Understood. Shall I comply with their requests?"

"Only the lawful ones. I have nothing to hide," she clarified for the benefit of their audience, "but I'm not about to give up my privacy unless they get a warrant. Besides, the station records are just going to corroborate whatever data you have, so it's pointless anyway." At least she hoped that was the case. She hated to think of all the ways her missing touchscreen could have been used without her knowledge.

"Understood."

"Good." Jorna stretched out her shoulders again. They'd grown tight as she rehashed everything with Savvy. "Now I'm not going to have much flexibility to work normally until this... situation is resolved. I'll need you to do some of the heavy lifting on my behalf."

Savvy was silent for a moment. "Query, Dr. Benton."

Jorna could just envision the exact degree of the automaton's head tilt. "Go ahead, Savvy."

"What heavy things would you like me to lift?"

A chuckle escaped Jorna, followed by a deeper laugh. Savvy's idiom filter still ran into trouble now and again, and the timing couldn't be better. Her amusement built until there were tears in her eyes. When had her life become so ridiculous?

"Dr. Benton?"

"All I meant, Savvy, is I'll be relying on your judgment as far as generating planting schedules and drone tasks while I'm being detained."

"Understood."

Jorna hoped so. She hoped for a lot of things, starting with Kaysar looking at her again like she was anything but a problem. But until Jorna cleared her name, being allowed to work remotely was the best she could hope for. She had no doubt Savvy would get things done even if it wasn't quite the way she would prefer.

That would have to be good enough, considering the circumstances.

8

JORNA SPENT A fitful night on the provided cot. First thing the following morning, two guards came to her cell to escort her to a conference room near the Bridge. That had to mean they'd made some kind of progress on the investigation, right?

Commander Kaysar was waiting for them. "Please wait outside unless called," she told the guards.

Jorna followed Commander Kaysar into the conference room. It could comfortably seat a dozen people, but right now it was just the two of them. The commander's perfume washed over Jorna. *Jasminum grandiflorum*. She inhaled deeply, the scent loosening some of the tightness in her chest. But Kaysar still hadn't looked at her properly, making it hard to read her mood.

Or glean why Jorna had been summoned here in the first place.

"We're going to hold our current position, delaying our arrival to the Dominican Republic," Kaysar told her.

That was certainly not ideal, although nothing about this situation was. "Long enough to get this situation resolved?"

Kaysar smiled thinly. "I've allotted a week. After that—"

"But our schedule—"

"You let me worry about the mission implications, Doctor."

Jorna was back to being called "Doctor" this morning, which didn't bode well. "This is something we should be deciding together," she said crossly. "If you don't trust me to do my job, then maybe you'd better return me to the brig."

The commander merely arched a brow. "That's not why you're here. Have you eaten?"

"Yes. A quick ration on my way over."

She made a face. "Hangry, then." She waved Jorna over to the console table laden with printed breakfast pastries and a caffeine station along the far wall. "Help yourself so we can get to work."

Jorna heaved a sigh at being chastened like a little kid, but maybe the extra calories would help her weather whatever task the commander had called her here for. She grudgingly selected a muffin and returned to the table. She supposed the fact that she still warranted a catering tray as though this was just another staff meeting was a good sign.

A smile touched Kaysar's eyes for a moment when she looked up from her touchscreen to confirm Jorna was eating something. Jorna's stomach fluttered, and it wasn't just the food. Well, not entirely. The commander still cared about her. After spending the night tossing and turning in the brig, that was a hopeful sign.

But after that brief crack in the commander's demeanor, it was back to business. "If we do have Supplicants on board, I think it's likely they took the place of one of the crew members."

Jorna recognized the tired cadence to Kaysar's words from many long nights spent in the lab. Jorna would bet money the commander never made it back to her quarters last night. "There was that new batch of trainees."

Kaysar nodded. "And the explosion not long after that. So I'm thinking we should go through the personnel files together." With a touchscreen, the commander displayed the list of crewmembers. The names hovered in the air on pinpoints of light projected from the center of the table. "Let's see if anyone matching you or your siblings' descriptions is among them."

Had the circumstances been different, Jorna could have kissed her for giving her something productive to do that contributed to the investigation instead of letting her continue to stew in the brig. But kissing was how they'd gotten into this mess in the first place, and Jorna had no idea how such an overture would be received after what happened. Would Kaysar see it as an attempt at manipulation, like Goh, or understand that the gratitude and no little desire Jorna felt had compelled her to reach out, despite all the reasons not to?

But at least they now had a concrete task they could focus on. *Together.* Jorna threw herself into the work as best she could under the circumstances. They went down the list of names in alphabetical order, clicking open each employee profile. "Next, next. No, no, no. Next. Wait. Go back." Kaysar obliged her and opened the record for Stirling Bertram. "Mid-thirties, Caucasian, brown eyes, black hair."

That would describe Eskil on paper, but the face looking back at Jorna was that of a stranger. "If the goal was to infiltrate the mission without me recognizing him, don't you think they would have colored his hair or gotten new irises or something?"

"You're the resident expert on Supplicants, not me."

A dubious honor. "It's just that if they went to such an extreme, I don't think they'd be so careless to let me ID them this easily. How many more do we have?"

"Four hundred and seventy-three."

Jorna groaned. "We need a better filtering criteria to narrow things down."

"Advances in body modification mean he may not look like your brother anymore," Kaysar pointed out.

"That's true, but I don't see Eskil or Karin making any permanent changes to their bodies. The same principles that make our work a sin make altering our bodies one as well."

"You can't defile your mortal vessel?"

"Exactly."

"What about vision or hearing loss?" There was genuine curiosity in the commander's voice instead of judgment.

"Glasses and other types of external aids are fine. Surgery to fix such things is not."

"What about heart disease or something?"

"God takes us on his terms. Trying to cheat death desecrates God's plans for us."

"So basically no alterations to the body, but most assistive devices are okay. Got it."

"There's a logic to it, but it's…"

"Pretty regressive."

"Yeah." The commander was watching Jorna again, and her face heated under her scrutiny. "What?" Jorna knew she sounded defensive, but she couldn't help it.

"It's just kind of amazing how you overcame such indoctrination."

Jorna grimaced. She didn't like thinking about just how easily she could have been trapped in such a life, how fortunate she'd been to find a way out. And now she was here. "Guess I've been lucky."

"Don't sell yourself short, Doctor. Independent thinking is one of the hardest qualities to cultivate in a world at odds with itself."

"Well, when you place as much stock in intellectual achievement as I have, anything that runs counter to that is a weakness. And in a fast-moving field such as mine, I can't help but feel like I'm still playing catch-up thanks to my stunted childhood. I can't help but wonder if I had a different upbringing, would I be even further along in my career."

"You can't let what-ifs rule your life."

"Contingencies were all I had for so long."

"Well, the secret's out," Kaysar said, not without sympathy. "Now you get to decide who you are without the weight of such a history holding you back."

Even now, despite everything that had happened, the commander still didn't blame Jorna for her upbringing. She remembered Danika's reaction when Jorna had finally told her the truth about her family. Danika had gone so very quiet, said she needed space for a few days. She'd come back, nearly a week later, but it had never been the same for Jorna after that.

Keeping her background hidden had become so ingrained, she never questioned it. She just assumed it was something to be ashamed of, something that made her unworthy somehow. She was still unworthy of Commander Kaysar's attentions, but not for the reason Jorna originally thought. The commander might be upset with Jorna for omitting the truth or for being so cautious when it came to her personal life, but those were her actions, not who she was as a person.

A distinction the commander was capable of making. A distinction Jorna had trouble making for herself. She still had a lot of growing up to do.

Jorna's wristcom chimed with an incoming message from Savvy. Holding back a sigh, she let it through. "What's up?"

"Dr. Benton, you wanted me to prepare the planting schedules for Tier 4."

"Right."

"Those are now ready. I've taken the liberty of sending them to your account."

"Thanks." Though why Savvy thought it necessary to call her to tell her of it was a bit puzzling. It wasn't like Jorna wouldn't see the plans when she checked her messages later. "Anything else?"

Savvy paused, no doubt processing Jorna's clipped tone and running any number of sub-routines to determine how to proceed. "I will begin working on the rest of my lifting routine for tomorrow."

Kaysar gave Jorna a puzzled look. "'Lifting routine'?"

"Just an inside joke. I told Savvy it would have to do a lot of the heavy lifting around the habitat while I was gone and, well..."

"I see." Kaysar smiled and took a sip of her coffee.

"I hoped it would cheer you up, Doctor." Savvy refrained from mentioning her bio markers this time, but Jorna didn't doubt the automaton already knew it had succeeded in boosting her mood.

"Thanks, Savvy. I'll keep an eye out for that drone schedule and check in with you later." She moved to terminate the call.

"Dr. Benton, query."

Jorna took a deep breath and sought patience. "What is it?"

"I was curious when you will be released."

There went Jorna's good mood. "Hopefully sooner rather than later."

"When you are, you should ask the commander to join you in the habitat. Didn't she say she was interested in seeing more of the temperate biomes?"

In an offhand comment on a conference call weeks ago. Something about missing home. Jorna exchanged a baffled look with Commander Kaysar. "I'm sure it'll happen at some point, but it's really not a priority at the moment."

"*Hemerocallis fulva* will be in bloom for only a few more days."

Jorna resisted the urge to roll her eyes. "That's great, Savvy. Now I really gotta run. Benton, out."

The commander watched Jorna over the rim of her

coffee mug. "Is Savvy always that… thorough?"

"Not usually. It was like it had forgotten our conversation last night." Something tickled the back of her brain, but she pushed off the sensation. "Maybe it just wanted confirmation before moving on. I did dump a lot of work on Savvy because of everything."

"I suppose questions are inevitable, AI or not."

Regardless, Savvy's call had accomplished one thing. The atmosphere between her and the commander wasn't as tense. Or at least Jorna was a bit more relaxed. Able to take a moment, look the commander in the eye, and tell her, "Thank you, by the way."

"For what?"

"For not treating me like a criminal." The commander had to follow procedure, but every step along the way, she'd tried to reassure Jorna the best she could, even if Jorna hadn't been able to appreciate it at the time.

Kaysar sighed and set her touchscreen aside. "You're no terrorist, Jorna." Her gaze turned distant. "I've seen all the different ways ideology can twist a person up, make them unrecognizable. You're nothing like that."

"When you were with Earth Shield?"

"Yes, but not just then. Bureaucrat, corporate shill, soldier, civilian, religious fanatic, eco-warrior—it's Kool-Aid all the way down. The only difference is which version you drink. I've come to believe all that really matters are which stances can be enforced by law or lawlessness or lack of will."

Jorna nodded. "Pick your poison. But there's something to be said for picking one that aligns with your values instead of uncritically accepting the one handed to you.

That's part of the reason why I've worked so hard to get here, the Climasphere, and be at the forefront of the work we do."

"We all did. And with any luck, we'll get to the bottom of this mess and get things back to normal now that we have a better sense of what we're up against."

"I hope it's as simple as you say," Jorna replied.

"I am very aware of what's at stake professionally and personally if we get this wrong."

Suddenly, the investigation was the last thing on Jorna's mind as she stared into Kaysar's eyes. *Ava*, she mentally corrected herself.

How Jorna wished none of this had happened. That she'd been brave enough to at least *try* to see if a relationship could be possible between them instead of burying herself in her work, beholden to an image of herself that had never been accurate in the first place. And now, with the truth out and her worst fears confirmed, all Jorna could think about was that night in the garden where none of this stuff had mattered. When this investigation was cleared up, where would that leave the two of them?

Jorna wanted to reach over and take the commander's hand in hers, to reassure them both they'd figure this out, all of it.

Before she could muster up the courage to do so, Kaysar looked away, as if reminding them both they needed to keep working, and picked up her touchscreen. "All right. No permanent body changes, but we can't rule out cosmetic ones. That still doesn't help us narrow things down, does it."

Jorna sighed as she forced herself to mentally shift

gears. "Maybe we're going about this the wrong way. My siblings won't have any idea how to do the work required of your crewmembers." Eskil and Karin weren't stupid—quite the opposite in fact—but if they'd remained a part of the church, they wouldn't even have a passing familiarity with most of the Climasphere's capabilities. "Or let's say they got enough training to fit in. That's not going to hold up, not once their mission or whatever gets underway. Let's cross-reference the profiles with supervisor reports."

"Anyone who's been tardy, absent, work not up to standards, you name it. Brilliant." The commander's hands skated over the touchscreen, inputting the new parameters. "Ooh. Here we go."

Four names flashed up on the projected display. Three men and one woman. The commander clicked on the woman's profile first.

"Well, I think we can safely eliminate her. She's nothing like my sister."

"Agreed, based on the images I was able to find on the network," Kaysar said. "Hmm... It looks like the only reason she came up was because she was late to her first shift. Attributed to seasickness. Next up, Jaxton Miller." They both stared at his photo. "He's tall enough."

"But those cheekbones... Ours could never look like that."

"Not without going under." Commander Kaysar looked up, giving Jorna a critical once-over that rooted her to the spot. "I like yours better anyway."

Kaysar's cheeks darkened as if she suddenly remembered why such banter between them was ill-advised. She scrolled through Miller's work record. "Hmm. Just one tardy for him too. A med tech."

Jorna did her best to push off her reaction to the compliment and tried to focus on Miller's face. "Wait a minute. That's the guy who made a hash of my IV yesterday. No, two days ago. I know Dr. Rafa has had them going through training all week, which doesn't leave a lot of time left over to hack the security feeds and plant explosives."

"I wouldn't think so, but you never know. Next up, Lazar Bakos. Definitely a maybe."

Jorna understood at once what she meant, given the man's height, weight, and hair color.

Kaysar moved on to the last name. "Then there's Andren Holt. Also on the maintenance team." She crossed her arms as she stared into the pixelated face. "Another maybe?"

Jorna stared at the image a beat longer, then blinked to ensure she wasn't imagining things. She stood and braced her hands on the table. "That's Eskil. I'm sure of it."

"I don't recall the reports saying your brother had blond hair or freckles like that."

"He doesn't. But that's definitely him." It was the eyes, so like her own staring back at her, that cinched it for her. In a black wig, the family resemblance would be undeniable. She didn't know whether to be relieved or not. Sure, they had a new suspect that wasn't her, but it was still her brother. Her own brother who'd put the Climasphere at risk.

And it would remain at risk until Eskil was found.

"This whole time I was hoping it wasn't anyone in my family. That this was one big misunderstanding." That it wasn't her fault. "If I'd known they were capable of doing something like this..."

Kaysar reached over and patted Jorna's shoulder. "You cannot keep punishing yourself for your family or your past. It's not fair to you or the life you've built for yourself."

Jorna wanted to believe her. She wanted to be the type of person who could simply live for herself without shame, brave enough to ask for what she wanted, starting with Commander Ava Kaysar.

Kaysar got to her feet. "I sent the shortlist to Goh as soon as it came in. Let's see how we did."

Jorna followed her into the hall, her steps more measured, hating that this brief respite with the commander was coming to an end, and that their respective duties would soon take over. But there was something Savvy had said earlier—

Kaysar turned to face her. "Well, aren't you coming?"

Jorna blinked, trying to battle back her distraction. "Yes, I…"

"What's wrong?"

"It's silly, but *Hemerocallis fulva*—what you might know as tiger lilies—aren't due to bloom for another month."

"AIs aren't infallible. Maybe Savvy got it mixed up with another plant. Ingested some bad training data at some point."

"Or maybe there's something off about that particular strain or the growing conditions or something I haven't even thought of yet."

"Does that happen often?" the commander asked.

"Contingencies I haven't thought of? Not usually."

"Hmm."

"What?"

"Have there been any other incidents or strange occurrences around the habitat?" Kaysar asked as they were admitted onto the Bridge.

"Besides my missing touchscreen?" Jorna raked her hands through her hair, suddenly exhausted. "It's hard to say with all the chaos of the harvest."

"All but Holt have been located and detained for questioning, Commander," Lieutenant Goh cut in.

"Work shift?" Kaysar asked.

"Never showed," Goh answered.

"Quarters?"

"Empty."

"Signal?"

"That requires your authorization."

"You have it."

Lieutenant Goh returned to the workstation to override privacy protocols in order to track Andren Holt's signal. The viewscreen displayed a layout of the entire sphere and zoomed in on one of the storage bays. Commander Kaysar exchanged a look with Lieutenant Goh, his hands already moving over the security workstation controls. "I'll get a team over there right away."

The commander looked at Jorna like she just realized she was still there. "We'll take it from here, but thank you for your assistance today. We'll be sure to reach out if we need to consult with you again," Kaysar said formally. "Go back to the habitat. It wouldn't be appropriate at this juncture to involve you any further in the investigation."

Jorna's ears grew hot. "So I'm being sidelined?" She hoped helping to narrow down the suspects proved she wasn't involved, but clearly they were still uncertain of her innocence. Officially at least, which was the only thing that counted.

The commander schooled her features quickly but not fast enough to hide the flash of guilt that swept over her face at Jorna's question. "If anything comes from this, we'll let you know."

Jorna swallowed an uncharitable response to that. She didn't want to make Kaysar's job harder. She was probably navigating reams of red tape as it was. "I'm going, but if you find Eskil, what are you going to do to him?"

"I know he's your brother—"

"That's not why I'm asking."

Kaysar squared her shoulders. "We'll interrogate him. Then keep him in the brig until we get guidance on how to proceed. Why do you ask?"

"He's a member of God's Supplicants. If the church hears about this, and they get involved, it will become a public relations nightmare with talk of religious liberties and discrimination."

"Thank you for your concern," the commander said flatly.

"Don't get me wrong," Jorna backpedaled. She'd only been trying to warn Kaysar, not tell her how to do her job. "If Eskil did this, he deserves to be punished. I just don't want this situation weaponized by the church."

"Your concern is noted, Doctor."

An alert blared from the security console. "That's the security team reporting in," Goh announced.

"On-screen."

The view of the ocean was replaced with drone cam footage of the security team. "Lieutenant, Commander, we followed the signal as requested," Officer Alvaro said.

"And?" Goh prompted.

"You'd better see for yourself."

The camera panned away from Alvaro's face and focused on a grubby corner of the cargo bay where a microchip tracker, devoid of the arm it had been dug out of, flashed up from a dark brown stain on the floor.

Commander Kaysar slammed her hand down on the edge of the workstation. "Dammit all. Make a note in the logs that we officially have a fugitive on board."

9

THE BRIDGE ERUPTED into movement and sound with the commander's pronouncement. Officers worked to coordinate with personnel throughout the Climasphere to set up a search for Andren Holt. Alvaro was still on the viewscreen making her report. The comms officer was compiling all available records while Goh started pulling surveillance feeds at the security workstation.

And Jorna... Jorna was in the way. *Go back to the habitat.*

"We'll need to run a sphere-wide heat scan and filter out all those with an associated signal to see if we can determine where he's hiding," Kaysar said.

"Done," Goh replied, "but it will take time."

Jorna didn't hear the commander's reply because she was already in the hall, flanked once more by the guards who'd accompanied her here that morning.

"We are your security detail for the rest of the day," the

first one said.

At least Commander Kaysar saw to that much before she'd dismissed Jorna. The firewall was no longer strictly necessary now that they had confirmed Eskil's presence on board, but that didn't change the fact she'd be woefully out of place if she remained on the Bridge.

Jorna wasn't sure what the protocol should be at a time like this, so she simply nodded at the officers assigned to her before making her way back to the habitat. They fell into step behind her, following at a distance where she could almost—*almost*—forget they were there. And why.

The habitat was supposed to be her domain, but even that didn't bring her the reassurance it usually did when they arrived. Everything rankled. Someone—most likely her brother—had attacked the Climasphere, taking everyone by surprise. None of her contingencies had prepared her for that or the sudden paranoia crawling through her despite the familiar surroundings.

First stop was her quarters, but when they entered, it was clear her rooms had been tossed. She glanced at the guards, who seemed just as surprised. "That's not your doing?"

They exchanged a confused look. "Not to our knowledge, Doctor."

Jorna sighed. Goh had probably seen to the honor himself. She quickly showered and pulled together an outfit from the clothes strewn about the floor. The mess would keep until she was certain Savvy had things under control. She headed over to the lab.

"Dr. Benton, you've returned," Savvy greeted her as the security officers took up positions around the room. It was stationed in front of the console for the habitat monitoring system. "Will the commander be joining us?"

"Not today. What's so important about her being here anyway?"

"The *Hemerocallis fulva* are blooming."

Jorna shook her head. "I think you've got your circuits crossed, Savvy. They're not due to bloom for another month or so. Have you run a diagnostic recently?"

"I am operating within acceptable parameters."

"Well, if you send a monitoring drone over to Tier 4, Quadrant 2, you'll see the tiger lilies aren't even close to flowering. How do you explain that?"

"I cannot, Dr. Benton."

She frowned. Could not or would not? Dread gathered in her gut. Maybe Eskil hadn't confined his tampering to just the research sector. "I think we'd better have Meigs take a look."

"I would be happy to send her a meeting request."

"No, I'll handle it."

"I insist—"

Jorna shook her head as she messaged Meigs on her wristcom. "Meigs, Benton here. Would you mind swinging by the lab? It seems Savvy—"

A crash sounded behind her, followed by a hollow thud. She whirled around in time to see the security guard closest to the door doubled over. Then Savvy struck him in the temple, knocking him out cold. What the hell?

Jorna could only stand there in disbelief as the other guard pulled out his sidearm and zapped Savvy, but the stun gun did nothing to slow it down. Savvy grabbed the guard with its powerful hands and slammed him against the back counter. He collapsed onto the floor, scattering sample plates for the gene sequencer.

"Benton? Benton?" Meigs squawked from her wristcom.

The engineer's voice pulled Jorna out of her stupor. Savvy had oriented on Jorna and was walking toward her, its eyes unnaturally bright. That wasn't good. The assistant pairing process could be undone with Jorna's consent, but she wasn't about to test that. She darted around Savvy, narrowly avoiding its swinging arms, and reached the charging station. She jabbed the button for the homing beacon. The signal could recall Savvy from any location on the Climasphere and still appeared to be in working order when Savvy stiffened then turned around at the summons. Once it returned to the charging station, docile once more, she slapped down the cage to keep it there.

"Benton?"

Jorna backed away from Savvy, not daring to look anywhere else as she brought the wristcom up to her mouth. "Meigs, I need you here pronto." She switched the channel over to the Bridge. "This is Dr. Jorna Benton with a medical emergency. Savvy just attacked my security detail." There was silence for a few seconds, then it sounded like the channel was routed up the chain of command. "Goh here. What's your status?"

As Jorna explained what happened, she could hear Kaysar swearing in the background. "I'm sending over the security footage." Lest they think *she* had put Savvy up to the attack.

"We'll get a medical team over there as soon as we can. Goh, out."

At least the guards were still breathing. Jorna dug

through the lab's emergency medical kit, keeping an eye on Savvy as she did so. Neither guard stirred as she bandaged their cuts and placed neural stabilizers on their temples. Hopefully that would be enough to tide them over.

Meigs showed maybe five minutes later. "What the hell happened here?" Her gaze landed on one of the unconscious guards. "Whoa."

"Savvy attacked them unprompted, and it was acting weird prior to that." Jorna got Meigs up to speed as she started unscrewing the fasteners to Savvy's chestplate. If Eskil could get to Savvy, nothing on the Climasphere was safe.

"It does look like Savvy's been tampered with," Meigs said around the penlight in her mouth as she examined the automaton's CPU.

"Just like the drones?"

Meigs paused to consider that. "Not quite, but who knows. I never did figure out which one of ours could have done it from the logs. You don't think—"

Jorna should have seen it sooner. "Our saboteur has been busy, it seems."

In moments, Meigs had diagnostic leads connected and the troubleshooting menu up and running on her touchscreen. "I think I flushed the malware out of its system. Thankfully, it was pretty rudimentary." She closed Savvy's carapace and booted it back up.

A happy little chime sounded, and Jorna struggled not to laugh at the incongruity. With everything going to shit around her, she couldn't afford to lose it.

Savvy blinked its eyes and looked at Jorna. "Dr. Benton, unit V6-128 reporting for duty."

"Savvy, do you recall what happened just before we shut you down?"

"Yes." Its head tilted to the side. "My primary functions were accessed and changed by... unknown. The new instructions were in conflict with my do-no-harm directive, but I was reprogrammed so I could not speak of the changes."

"But you tried to tell me all the same, didn't you. The little mistakes, the insistence on the commander's presence."

Savvy's eyes flashed. "I hoped one of you would take notice before something happened. I am sorry."

Breath gusted out of Jorna. She was partly to blame as well. If she hadn't been so distracted, she would have put all the clues together much, much sooner. "We'll get it sorted. Don't worry."

In the meantime, she needed to make sure nothing else in the sphere had been tampered with. She went over to her workstation and started scanning the readouts for all the sensors and cameras stationed throughout the habitat. "Savvy, have you noticed any strange readings?"

"No. The automated monitoring system is operating within acceptable parameters."

"You think there's more?" Meigs asked, looking at the screen over Jorna's shoulder.

"I think we were so busy cleaning up after the harvest we missed the signs there was something else going on around here. I don't want to overlook anything else."

"Incoming message from Commander Kaysar," Savvy announced.

"Let it through."

"Channel open."

"What's your status?" Commander Kaysar asked.

"I've stabilized the injured guards, but they need more help than we can give them. Meigs is here now, and she helped me out with Savvy."

"More sabotage?"

"That's what we suspect. And unless Goh authorized a search of my quarters—"

The entire room shuddered. Dozens of alarms pierced the air, the competing sounds emitting from the workstation and both Jorna's and Meigs's wristcoms. Meigs shouldered Jorna aside, her hands a blur over the workstation controls, and swore. "Whatever that was just deployed the emergency bulkheads for the habitat."

That meant no one in or out until they were retracted. It was supposed to protect the plants if the sphere ever took on water, but now they were trapped inside.

"Commander?" Were the commlines down too? Or worse, had they been caught up in the explosion as well? Jorna didn't breathe as one second passed, then another. This wasn't it. It couldn't be. "Ava, are you still there?"

"Yes, Dr. Benton. We're still here." Jorna nearly sagged with relief. The commander sounded distracted, though, and no wonder. "Things holding on your side, I presume?"

"As far as we can tell," Meigs said.

"Good. Unfortunately, that explosion's going to delay the medical team we promised you. The transponder with the mainland is also down. And I have more bad news. The heat scan of the work ring just completed, and it shows there are no unaccounted-for crewmembers on board."

"But if he's not there, that means…"

Eskil was somewhere in the habitat. Jorna's stomach burned at the thought.

"We're working on different solutions to get a security team over to you, but in the meantime, I want you to secure what you can, retreat to your safe room, and await reinforcements."

Jorna shook her head. "That leaves too much time where things can go wrong."

"Wait. Let the security team check things out first, then—"

"The habitat is my responsibility, Commander. And if it is my brother…" She blew out a breath. "Maybe I can find a way to talk him down."

"It's too dangerous. I've dealt with these types of fanatics before. They can't be reasoned with. Only consequences get through to them, and even that's not a guarantee."

"Then stop arguing with me and figure out a way to get over here to help while I play for time." It was so clear to Jorna what needed to be done. She didn't understand why the commander was fighting her on this.

"Benton—Jorna—think about this a moment. What if he's *trying* to draw you out? If we lose you… You don't have to prove anything to me or—"

"But I still need to prove something to myself."

"Dammit, Jorna. Listen to me—"

Her voice turned crackly, then a screech of static flooded the line.

"Commander, are you there? Commander?"

Savvy's head tilted to the side. "It appears the signal frequency has been jammed."

"Great. Just what we need." Jorna turned to Meigs. It was

just the two of them, up against whatever Supplicant bullshit Eskil had up his sleeve. Meigs seemed to realize that as well, the fine lines around her mouth pulled tight with worry. "I'll see what I can do to get those bulkheads retracted while you check out the generators. If someone's tampered with them—"

"I got the picture, believe me." Meigs started collecting her tools.

Massive amounts of electricity had to be generated to support the habitat's electroculture gradient, the drones, and the supercomputers that helped run everything else. Jorna didn't think nonspecialists had a chance to breach the area, but she couldn't afford to be wrong. She couldn't afford *any* more mistakes. Even if it meant splitting up with Meigs.

"Be careful. Anything remotely out of place, I want you to wait for backup. Otherwise secure the area like the commander said."

"Will do."

As Meigs headed out, Jorna fought off the panicky flood of adrenaline in her system. Jorna didn't know what she'd just asked of the chief engineer, but Meigs understood what her responsibilities were. All Jorna could do was leave her to it, so she could see to her own responsibilities.

Easier said than done, she thought grimly as Savvy stared at her with its unblinking eyes. "You coming with?"

"Without a full diagnostic, I cannot be certain there are no more executables hidden in my programming."

"We'll take our chances. Move."

Jorna jogged out of the lab. With blood beating in her ears, she could barely hear Savvy scuttling behind her to catch up as they headed to the corridor that connected the habitat to the work ring.

When they arrived, the bulkheads created an iron wall prohibiting any access to the shuttle platform and the rest of the Climasphere. The controls had definitely been tampered with. Electrical components looked like they had been yanked out of the panels by a toddler on a rampage.

"Savvy, I want you monitoring the tiers until we can get the feeds displayed." Then she consulted her wristcom. "Meigs? It's Benton."

"Here."

Jorna stared down helplessly at the nest of wires and couplings below. She'd been cross-trained on a number of tasks, but electrical repair hadn't been one of them. "You're not going to like what's been done to your electronics. You'll need to talk me through what I need to do to restore the command pathway for the bulkheads."

Meigs swore.

"Dr. Benton." Savvy's eyes flashed as it consulted the thousands of cameras and data feeds throughout the habitat. "There appears to be a dark area on Tier 3. A number of cameras in Quadrant 1 are nonresponsive."

The Climasphere was going dark bit by bit, and Jorna was still no closer to stopping it from happening. "Then that's where we're headed next. Meigs, stand by."

"Query. How will you stop the perpetrator?" Savvy asked as it trundled after her.

"I only need to slow him down long enough for the security team to get here." A simple enough goal, she hoped, as the hangar grumbled around them. More explosions? Or perhaps it was simply the sea taking advantage of any hull damage. Jorna's lungs squeezed. No good could come from thinking about the shear stress on the sphere right now.

In the hangar, Jorna pulled on her biosuit and got the skiff ready to fly. A light drizzle pattered down on Jorna's suit and Savvy's silver carapace. She hadn't anticipated that—it had been well over twenty-four hours since she'd laid eyes on a weather forecast for the habitat.

When they reached Tier 3, Jorna activated her visor and panned across a plot of swamp tupelos. "I don't see any obvious damage from up here. Did the feeds go down one by one or all together?"

"All together." Savvy's eyes flashed. "There's another outage on Tier 5, Quadrant 3."

"Just now?"

"Yes." Savvy sent the coordinates to the navigation panel.

She directed the skiff to a section of the temperate forest tier, practically on the opposite side of the sphere. The rain curtained down around them, narrowing Jorna's field of vision to just a few feet in front of the skiff, but at least it shrouded the ocean, lurking below, from view. They were nearly there, according to the instruments, when Savvy announced, "Now there are outages on Tier 4, Quadrant 2 and Tier 7, Quadrant 4—"

"This is ridiculous." Jorna could barely see at this point. She pulled up on the steering wheel, dragging the craft up even higher to escape the rain clouds. The console bleated a warning.

"We are approaching the upper limit of the gravity tolerance for the craft," Savvy reported.

"So noted," Jorna bit out.

"Query. What are you—"

"Hang on."

The rain finally stopped, and Jorna could see again thanks to the sunlight shining down on the dome through a break in the clouds. Squinting, she was able to identify the locations of the various outages, perfectly spread around the habitat like numbers on an analog clock. "We've been had, Savvy."

"I do not understand."

"This is just a ruse. To bring us out into the open or to pull us away from the work areas. But why?" She glanced around like she had a target on her back. In this case, a literal one. But there were only her plants spread out on the tiers below and the glare off the sea.

Something dark and unnatural-looking showed up against the white of the snow on Tier 9. "There. I want to get a closer look at Quadrant 2." She maneuvered the skiff over.

"Shall I join you?"

"No. I want you to stay here, ready to meet me in a hurry."

"Understood." Savvy synched with the craft controls. "Standing by."

"Wish me luck." Jorna hopped off the skiff and onto the tier, jogging as fast as her biosuit allowed toward deep gouges in the sedge along the rim. It looked like someone had purposefully dragged their heels through the delicate grass. Against the snow, the exposed and battered sedge was almost obscene, a wound that hurt to look at.

Every specimen in the upper tiers required far more time to grow and mature, even in an accelerated growth environment like the Climasphere. Jorna's stomach ached at the damage. She would have benched one of her horticulture techs for the rest of the mission if something like this had happened on their watch.

But this was her watch. Hers and hers alone.

Something slammed into her helmet, so hard her visor shattered and her ears rang with alarms from the broken seal. What just happened? She squinted against the glare of the dome, unable to focus on anything.

Savvy. She needed Savvy. Blearily, she brought her wristcom up to her face. "Savvy, where are you?" She could only manage a weak rasp.

"Approaching your location."

"Good. That's... good."

She dragged herself upright, and the entire side of her face erupted in pain. With a harsh cry, she spun around. There, like a funhouse mirror reflection of himself, stood Eskil, brandishing a spanner.

She thought she was prepared to see him again, but it was still a shock after all these years. She held out her hands, the need to protect herself at war with the automatic urge to draw her brother into her arms for a hug no matter all the things he'd done to bring the Climasphere to ruin. "Whatever it is you're planning, whatever you hope to accomplish..."

The dye was fading from Eskil's hair, and the freckles were no more. A crude bandage was wrapped around his forearm where he'd dug out the tracker. For him to have gone to such extremes against the tenets of his faith... Eskil was no longer the little kid she'd read adventure stories to after school.

"Good to see you too, sis."

Whatever hope she had of talking things out died at the breathtaking animosity in her brother's gaze, but she had to try. She owed them both that much.

"You went to great lengths to lure me out here. Why?"

Instead of answering, he came at Jorna again. They were practically the same size now, something her mind struggled to account for as they grappled. She twisted away but still got walloped with the spanner across her ribs. She yelped as the pain blazed up her side, bringing tears to her eyes.

A blurry image of her brother stepped into view and pulled something metallic and gun-shaped from his coveralls. She pushed off her helmet and swung it wildly, catching Eskil in the face.

He spat out a bloody tooth. "I didn't plan on eliminating you myself, but I think I'll make an exception."

Icy fingers of fear stabbed through Jorna. "Whatever happened to 'Thou shalt not kill'?"

"Godless heretics don't count, Jorna. You know that."

The same bullshit. She knew better than to reason with such fanaticism. But she had to play for time.

"Karin thought I was worth saving."

Eskil's face screwed up. Clearly he and Karin had argued on that point before. "She was misguided. She's learned her lesson." The smirk on his lips sent alarm bells through Jorna.

"What did you do?"

He lifted a shoulder. "For communicating with someone expelled from the church, she was sent home in disgrace to atone. As it was, she nearly blew the entire operation."

Jorna supposed she should feel grateful Karin had felt some duty toward her before sabotaging everything she'd worked so hard for, but it only highlighted the magnitude of how spiritually corrupt the Supplicants had become, her blood family in lockstep with them.

"And we couldn't have that now, could we." Eskil waved the gun this way and that.

"I just assumed she was in on it. This"—Jorna gestured to Eskil—"and the attack on the shipyard."

"You've been away from the church too long. There's a lot more of us now, and we've got so many plans. Divine plans." He took a step toward her. "Now it's your turn to be punished."

She held out her hands. "You can't be serious." Apprehension inundated her. Along with anger. So much of it she'd kept bottled up for far too long. How dare he judge her? "You destroy the Climasphere, you'll never find the paradise you've been looking for."

"I don't do this for me but all the others." His eyes drifted closed as he lifted his chin, a beatific look on his face. "May the meek inherit the Earth from my actions this day." Then he took aim.

Her vision constricted around the gun pointing at her, her breath locking in her lungs at the uncertainty of what came next. All her plans were in shreds. Her hopes...

Eskil's fingers twitched, and his gaze cut away from her to something in the distance. Then she heard it. The skiff's automated high-altitude warnings announced its arrival before it emerged from the clouds. She still had some hope left. Savvy wheeled the craft around, hovering right below the lip of the tier, so Jorna only had to step into it.

Using what little energy she had left, Jorna threw herself toward the skiff as the gun went off. The bullet shattered the windshield as she rolled across the running boards and slammed into Savvy's legs.

"You still alive in there, Jorna?"

Damn it all. Jorna didn't answer—she didn't trust herself not to react to Eskil's mocking tone and remained crouched on the floor of the skiff.

"Any word from the Bridge?" she whispered to Savvy.

"Communications are still down, Dr. Benton. You are without your helmet. Do you require medical attention?"

"I'll be fine, Savvy."

The craft swayed as Savvy pulled away from the tier—the repulsors weren't as effective this high up. She risked a glance over the railing and caught a glimpse of snowy footprints darting through a plot of bearberries. Jorna tracked the path of destruction with her eyes until it caught up with her brother where he stood, staring at the skiff.

Eskil's mouth was still bleeding, but he inexplicably grinned as he met Jorna's gaze. "You can't escape, Jorna. No one can. Your sins will be your end."

Jorna shook her head. Supplicant doctrine was no longer the metric she used to measure her life. It had already stunted her sense of self, keeping people at arm's length. If she got through this, she wouldn't let the Supplicants' twisted view of the world take anything else from her.

Eskil raised his wristcom to his lips, speaking some command Jorna was too far away to hear. Then he scrambled over the side and down onto the next tier. What now?

Jorna had to believe the cavalry was coming—Commander Kaysar would see to it somehow. And yet her gut twisted at the grin on her brother's face, his eyes wide, almost manic.

"I don't like this," Jorna muttered. "Get Meigs on the line."

"Of course, Dr. Benton. Line open."

And it was catching the chief engineer mid-swear. That boded well.

"What's your status, Meigs?"

A crash sounded somewhere in the engineer's vicinity. "You tell me. What the hell just happened up there?"

"My... The saboteur and I got into it, but he's stranded on Tier 8."

"Not the humans. I'm talking about the drones," Meigs said as if Jorna was stupid.

What did she mean *the drones*? Then Jorna understood all too well as one of the air scrubbers slammed into the hull of the skiff. The craft juddered, and Jorna narrowly avoided getting hit with a face full of debris. Busted components smoked and crackled as they flew by her. Savvy didn't fare as well, its head and torso getting pelted as it kept the skiff pointed at the hangar, still too many kilometers away.

Before Jorna could take a breath, another one hit, this one a much smaller monitoring drone. It smashed into the hull, skidded twice, then broke up against the windshield.

"You have homicidal drones down there too?"

"Ding ding ding. I was able to deactivate a couple and shut the blast doors surrounding the core but—" Meigs was interrupted by a painful metal squeal.

A surge of adrenaline rushed through Jorna. "Tell me those aren't the augers."

"They started boring through the doors." Meigs sounded

almost punchy. "It'll take hours, but there's enough of them to get the job done."

And with the lines of communication severed, who knew how long Meigs would need to stay holed up before security could offer their assistance.

Another monitoring drone buzzed past Jorna's ear. Way too close.

"We need to implement a system-wide shutdown," Meigs shouted to be heard over the background noise.

The drone broke apart on the running boards by Jorna's feet. "Agreed. Stand by."

Dark shadows swirled in the clouds off the right-hand side of the skiff. More rain? The undulating shapes resolved into a phalanx of pollinator drones, heading straight for them.

Shit.

"Savvy, reroute my workstation access to the skiff's console," Jorna demanded. "And where did you stash that restrainer Meigs gave me?"

"One moment, Dr. Benton."

It engaged the skiff's autopilot and retrieved the restrainer from the emergency kit strapped to its shoulders. Jorna's hands closed over the device gratefully.

The skiff's speed hadn't changed, but the pollinator drones were gaining on them. From the opposite direction, another air scrubber angled toward them, picking up speed. Blasted things. She zapped it when it got close, and it dropped out of the sky.

She made her way over to the skiff's console. "This is Dr. Jorna Benton, Principal Scientist of the Climasphere, authorizing the complete shutdown of the automated drone monitoring system."

VOICE IDENTITY, VERIFIED.

She pressed her palm down on the scanner.

BIOMETRIC IDENTITY, VERIFIED.

Next, a security question flashed on the screen:

WHAT IS YOUR FAVORITE FLOWER?

A low hum was her only warning before a pollinator drone's tendril-like injectors wrapped around her face. She wrestled with the contraption as it probed her ears and nose, tightening its grip on her head and neck like an octopus its prey.

She slammed her head against the console once, then a second time, the crunch and whine of components telling her she'd finally done enough damage to pry the damn thing off her. Just in time to use the restrainer on two more drones approaching the skiff.

The security question still flashed on the screen. "Jasmine," Jorna gasped. "*Jasminum grandiflorum.*"

A long pause followed in which Jorna envisioned the complete and total annihilation of the Climasphere, all because she couldn't remember the exact phrasing she'd used originally.

SECURITY QUESTION, VERIFIED. DOES THE CHIEF ENGINEER CONCUR?

"Yes," Meigs said tersely.

SHUT DOWN COMMENCING IN 3, 2, 1...

Two spot irrigator drones collided with the skiff. Their tanks exploded on impact. Water slapped down on the console, sending up a cascade of sparks.

"We are losing altitude," Savvy announced quite unnecessarily as the skiff shuddered and tilted down toward the ground. They really needed to work on that.

More drones pelted the hull, and another explosion rocked the vehicle. Acrid smoke stung Jorna's eyes. A metallic howl sent the skiff plummeting toward the tiers below, and she could do nothing but hang on.

10

JORNA WASN'T SURE how long it took for the haze of pain to recede so she could focus on the spidery limbs of the adolescent oak trees overhead. They were common to a number of different biomes scattered throughout the habitat and across elevations as well. All she could smell was smoke and scorched metal and burnt plastic. Savvy, the skiff...

The crash rewound with harsh clarity in her mind's eye.

She lay there, dazed for a long moment, then shook off the agony of what was probably a significant head injury. Then, forcing back a groan, she pulled herself to her feet. Something pretty vital had snapped in her right arm, and she limped over to where the skiff had plowed into the tier, uprooting dozens of saplings and what looked to be *Cephalotaxus harringtonii*. Japanese plum-yew.

That helped narrow things down. Tier 4 or Tier 5.

"Savvy?"

No answer.

The automaton lay in a crumpled heap where it had been ejected from the skiff, but otherwise appeared intact. Jorna struggled to turn it onto its back. One of its legs was missing, and the opposite hand was canted up at an awkward angle. Its chestplate was cracked in a couple places. Savvy's eyes slowly focused on Jorna's face.

"Shut ddddowwwnnn of the autoautoautomated drone system was successfulllllll."

Sure enough, she could make out a silvery line of drones in the distance, snaking their way back toward the Hive. One less thing to worry about. For now.

"What's your status, Savvy?" She was almost afraid to ask.

"My physiiiisicalll forrrrrmmmm needsss to be be be repaired, but Iiiiiii am fine."

"You did good, Savvy. We'll make sure you go straight to the top of the repair list after this." If not Meigs, someone else from the sphere, Jorna would make sure of it.

"Thhaaankkk you you you you, Dr. Bennnnntonnnnnnn."

Those echoes were getting old fast. "Blink twice if comms are still down."

Savvy blinked twice.

"Okay. I want you to keep broadcasting in case they can receive us even if we can't receive them, got it?"

Another double-blink.

"Tell them..." Jorna bit her lip. "Tell Commander Kaysar she was right about my brother."

Jorna couldn't pretend any longer this wasn't personal. She had drawn her brother here as surely as the Climasphere's mission had. This was her mess to clean up.

One of Savvy's servos made a pitiful whine as it tried and failed to sit up. "Where arrrre you gogogogoing?"

"Don't worry. I'm going to put a stop to this once and for all."

Eskil had already hijacked the drone monitoring system. What more was he capable of? They couldn't risk underestimating him again. *She* couldn't. And with comms down and no clear sense of how long they'd be cut off from the rest of the sphere... Time was not on their side.

If she played it safe while her brother was running loose and the worst came to pass, she'd never forgive herself.

Savvy pointed to a spot behind her. The medkit from the emergency bag lay on the ground a few meters away. Jorna got a lump in her throat. Even now, the automaton was trying to take care of her.

"Thanks, Savvy. We'll get this figured out. I promise."

From the pack, Jorna stabbed a pain relief medipen into her thigh and bandaged her arm to her side so it wouldn't swing as she walked around. Her jaw relaxed for the first time since she woke up as the drugs entered her system. She'd wrenched her ankle pretty good too, but she'd manage. She had to.

Lieutenant Goh had been right, as well. Jorna *hadn't* done enough to protect the mission. If she'd been more forthcoming sooner... The important thing now was she had a chance to make up for that.

The waning afternoon sun helped orient Jorna to her location relative to where she last saw Eskil. She continued clockwise around the tier until she came upon what she was looking for: a recessed tool shed built into the side of the upper tier. They were all numbered, and this one confirmed she'd found herself in one of the temperate forest quadrants on Tier 5 even though she'd yet to clear the plot of oak trees to confirm it.

Inside, she commandeered a hover cart and steered it toward the dedicated cart path that cut across this section of tiers to provide easy access to the nearest storage bay. Back up to Tier 8 where she last saw her brother. She punched the accelerator as far as it would go, and it responded with a surprising burst of speed. She'd only been on one of these things loaded down with specimens and equipment, never an empty cargo bed rattling behind her. The unchecked speed prompted an alarm as she zoomed up the cart path.

"Warning: This vehicle has reached an unsafe speed. Please slow down. Warning…"

There was no way to deactivate the damn thing, so she just grit her teeth as the cart continued to climb. Assuming Eskil was familiar with the layout of the habitat, which seemed a given at this point, he'd know the only way back to the work areas surrounding the habitat was through the hangar or one of the storage bays. With the cart speeding her along, Jorna hoped she'd be able to head off Eskil before he could do any more damage.

The cart reached the taiga biome on Tier 8, shuddering in protest at the hard right turn Jorna made to exit the path. It had recently snowed up here, maybe that morning, but no footsteps interrupted the ground. She continued on, scanning the tier.

Ten minutes later, she glimpsed a trail of footprints and slowed down slightly as she maneuvered the cart past a row of delicate cloudberries to follow. The footprints continued clockwise along the tier, past plots of fir, pine, and spruce. Jorna parked the hover cart and activated its emergency beacon. Her ankle protested as she got out. She searched for anything that might serve as a weapon and settled on a good-sized branch that had fallen. It felt like another lifetime when she had played knights in the woods back home with Eskil and Karin in one of their rare free moments not spent on chores or scripture, brandishing sticks in mock-sword fights, smiting unbelievers.

And now it had come to this.

"Not another step, Jorna."

She turned around stiffly. There was Eskil, gun in hand. Dammit. He'd gotten behind her somehow. Distraction, delay... That was still the plan.

"What's wrong?" he mocked. "This not the family reunion you were hoping for?"

She grit her teeth and redoubled her grip on the tree branch. It didn't feel nearly enough. "There's still a way out of this if you stop now."

"Stop?" he said with a snort. "Never. But don't worry. I'm not going to kill you. I've decided I want you to see this abomination sink into the ocean first." He kept the gun aimed at her as he pulled a piece of plastipaper grimy from handling out of his pocket. "Now you're going to take me here."

It was a crude drawing for the electrical access panels throughout the habitat. They weren't far from the one for this tier, which he pointed to with a stubby index finger. His hands looked so much like Dad's hands, it pulled the air out of her lungs.

Then he grabbed the branch from her, jerking her injured arm in the process, and tossed it aside. "Let's go."

She walked ahead of him as best she could, and when she couldn't, he prodded her with the gun to keep her moving.

"Why did you do it? Why did you come?" Jorna asked over her shoulder.

"We hoped to scuttle the launch entirely, but we ran into trouble and had to improvise."

"So you found a way to infiltrate the crew."

He nodded. "But I'd like to think we made up for lost time."

She turned around. "We?"

Eskil just grinned like he'd gotten away with something. And he had. She never would have thought him capable of any of this.

Jorna swore under her breath as she resumed her march. "You can't tell me it was just the Climasphere you were after. You came here to teach me a lesson."

"Do you have any idea what it was like for us when you left? What it was like for *me*? Everyone watching and waiting for us to fall just like you did." He spoke harshly, each word costing him. "So much scrutiny, so much pressure to be perfect Supplicants lest your shame reflect poorly on us. But now there won't be any more doubts."

They reached the electrical access panel, a squat gray metal cabinet up against the inner wall of the tier.

"Open it."

He needed her credentials to do so. She had to stall him as long as she could. "What on earth for?"

"We're going to overload the gradient."

"There are redundancies and fail-safes—"

"Not if I already disabled them," he said in a sing-song voice. "And if not, I have this." He brandished a brick-like device that he must have had hidden away in one of his pockets. Her heart kicked into overdrive at the sight. Was it some kind of bomb like he used on the research lab? Hate had driven her brother to destroy her plants, the habitat, the entire sphere if he could manage it. A crusade she feared he'd never relinquish, but she had to try to keep him talking. She owed it to everyone who believed in the Climasphere's mission, and she owed it to herself, too, for the future she had always wanted. "You compromised your own beliefs to come here, and now your actions will only hurt the cause you claim you care so much for. Don't you see? Whatever else you have planned for us *has* to end."

"No. I'm here to restore our family's honor. Be glad the Benton family will live on, inspiring a new era of God's Supplicants everywhere."

Such delusion was breathtaking. Commander Kaysar was right. Jorna couldn't fight it—there was too much there. She could only mourn it and move on. "I should have tried harder to get you out. I'm sorry I let you down."

"Sorry?" Eskil snarled, the gun trembling in his hand. "You think I *wanted* to follow in your footsteps? Everything I thought you were was a lie. Our family's greatest shame."

"I'm not the one planning to murder hundreds of innocent people."

Jorna searched Eskil's face, desperate for any sign of the little boy who used to look up at her like she could do anything. But their shared past was long behind them now, the way back thorny with betrayal.

On both sides.

"I refuse to believe your god would forgive such a thing," she said stubbornly.

"Innocent or guilty, it doesn't matter. I do this not for myself but all who come after. May their hands remain clean, their souls untainted by the evil you've wrought here."

"The only evil here is what you smuggled on board."

"Lies! No matter how many plants you grow, how many get reestablished on Earth, no matter how much you try, you will *never* measure up to God's divinity." He shook his head, his shoulders shaking with wheezing laughter. "You think this place is a beacon for humanity? Please. I've seen that drab dorm you're living in."

Of course he had. But the thought of Eskil in her quarters, unbeknownst to her, made her flinch at the renewed sense of violation.

He sneered, transforming the smears of blood on his face into a macabre mask. "I've seen you too, Jorna. Scurrying around, no better than a glorified groundskeeper, and for what? No friends, no family, just a blaspheming robot and your plants, and even those I'm going to take away."

His frank assessment stung, but she also knew he couldn't begin to conceive of a life of inquiry, of service, of the affirmation that comes from working with people with the same goals, same values, same determination to do what they could for a brighter future.

He jabbed the gun into her side, casting aside such thoughts. "Now get that panel open."

She reluctantly stepped forward and punched in the access code with her left hand. A series of clicks followed, and the door swung open, revealing the switchboard for the entire tier.

"Turn it off."

She made a show of trying to flip one of the switches. "I can't. I don't have the strength with my left hand." Her injured right arm still hung lifelessly at her side.

Eskil heaved a sigh. "Fine. I'll do it. Move."

Jorna took one step back, then another, knowing she only had one chance to get this right.

Her brother fired two shots into the panel. Burnt plastic filled her nose as smoke fountained out. Grinning at the destruction, her brother tucked the gun into his belt and started pulling the board apart with his hands. She bent down, scooped up a handful of snow, and launched it at the panel. Eskil cursed as some of it sprayed into his face. The rest of it melted instantly.

"What are you—"

No. No more. This ended now. Without letting herself think, Jorna lunged for Eskil, pushing him into the panel. As he made contact, he arched back as if someone's icy fingers trailed down his spine, his face a rictus of pain.

Jorna eased his spasming form down to the ground and took the gun from him. Then she stood back, quivering. Her suit had protected her from the electric shock, but it couldn't protect her from the wounded look on her brother's face that had swiftly contorted into hate.

She stared down at the gun in her hands, her trembling, uncertain fingers not at all familiar with the language of violence. She inwardly quailed. What next? How far would she have to go?

Then, the familiar hum of repulsor lifts filled the air.

Jorna didn't dare breathe past the bubble of anticipation in her throat. Eskil's feverish gaze went to the air skiff hovering somewhere behind her.

Security officers emerged from the trees. Jorna barely had the chance to back away and pass off the gun to someone way more qualified to handle it before her brother was surrounded. She pointed one of the security officers to the explosive device that had fallen to the ground in front of the access panel during the scuffle before limping over to Commander Kaysar's skiff.

The commander's gaze swept over her, lingering on Jorna's face for a long moment. The afternoon sky haloed Commander Kaysar, setting off red and gold highlights in her hair as she stood there, fully in control of the situation. "All right, Doctor?"

Jorna managed a nod. A piss-poor handoff to be sure, but she was too worn out to care about the particulars at this point. She'd done her part as best she could. Kaysar would do the same.

It seemed like the commander wanted to say something more, but there was no time, not given their audience. "See to her injuries," she said to the med tech who'd accompanied them.

Two security officers had gotten Eskil to his feet, but her brother's reaction time was significantly delayed as he was frog-marched on board the skiff. He swayed on his feet as he was checked over for weapons, swimming in and out of awareness.

Kaysar addressed him. "Eskil Benton, you are under arrest by the authority placed in me by the United Nations. Do you understand?"

With an almost dreamy look on his face, Eskil gazed off into the distance as if he was supremely unconcerned with his situation. The security officers kept their rifles trained on him as Goh got the skiff underway.

Commander Kaysar's jaw worked as she took a step toward Eskil. "We know your plan was to sneak on board and frame your sister for the destruction of the Climasphere. We've already detained your confederate."

This elicited a flash of disbelief, and Eskil finally deigned to look at Commander Kaysar for a moment before he faced the railing, his mouth hardening. Jorna had seen that expression one too many times to know he had no intention of complying with whatever was asked of him if he could help it.

Commander Kaysar met Jorna's gaze, seemingly asking, "Well?" with her eyes. Jorna could only shrug her non-injured shoulder in response. Eskil was no longer the brother she knew, let alone recognized. She hissed as the tech sprayed wound-heal onto her cheek.

One of the officers produced a pair of handcuffs, but Eskil collapsed to the floor of the craft with a weak wheeze before they could secure them. As though he'd expended all his reserves in facing the commander and had nothing left over, not after what happened.

Not after what Jorna did to him.

"He was shocked pretty badly by the electroculture gradient," Jorna explained. It was the only way she could think of to stop him without killing him. And she still wasn't certain she'd succeeded, based on the gray cast to his skin as he lay there.

Kaysar directed the med tech to cease his work on Jorna

and take a closer look at her brother. After taking his vitals, the tech cut open his coveralls to place stickipads across his torso for an EKG reading.

Eskil groaned and tried to push the medical equipment away. "What's going to happen to me?"

"After what you've done, I can't promise much," Kaysar replied, "but I can promise your safe return to the mainland, where you will be brought to account for your crimes. And if there's legal counsel or a trusted spiritual advisor you wish to consult back home, we'll do our best to make that possible."

Eskil turned to Jorna. The dazed look in his eyes had vanished, same with his helpless demeanor. "Let them renounce me," he rasped. "My conscience is clear, sister. Is yours?"

Before she could formulate a response, before the guards could even react, Eskil exploded to his feet and shoved the tech into the guards standing watch. Then he bolted toward her and slammed her against the railing. Air whooshed out of her lungs, and stars danced in her eyes. She heard shouts of alarm, saw Kaysar's shocked face for the briefest of instants, before he tightened his hold on her and pitched them both over the side of the skiff with a surprising burst of strength.

Time seemed to slow down as they plunged toward the sea. Jorna's mind struggled to make sense of it all as her brother clung to her like a busted pollinator drone. Every time she managed to pull one of his limbs off her, another would take its place, binding them so thoroughly, it was as though he wanted to ensure they'd face final judgment together.

She was screaming when they hit the water, Eskil's feverish recitation of the Lord's Prayer ringing in her ears. The shock of the impact finally forced them apart, and she jackknifed into the chilly depths. Her brother was somewhere above her, but she lost track of him as she thrashed toward the surface. But it didn't matter how hard she kicked, how long her lungs burned for air. The ocean tightened its hold on her, and her limbs grew heavier and heavier as water flooded her battered biosuit.

Oh *god*.

A paralyzing sort of panic gripped her as she was forced to live out one of her nightmares in real time. When the oceans rose and pulled her under with unstoppable force. Her stomach heaved. She couldn't fall into the sea and let that be the end of it. She had to keep going. Black dots filled her vision as she forced off one suit sleeve and clawed at the other. She kicked out, dislodging the pant legs so she could shimmy out of the rest of it. The last of her breath bubbled out of her mouth, leaving her more alone than she'd ever been her whole life. She kicked, and kicked...

And still the surface shimmered out of reach.

A shadow fell over her, and she despaired that the darkness had finally come for her like it always did in her dreams. Something grabbed hold of one arm, then the other, yanking her upward. Lieutenant Goh and another member of the security team pulled her sputtering out of the sea. Jorna coughed and spit out saltwater and did it all over again before she registered the fact that she was alive, she was breathing, and she was safe on the air skiff, Commander Kaysar on one side and a med tech drying her off with an emergency blanket on the other.

"Ava?"

"Shh. I'm here." Kaysar squeezed Jorna's uninjured hand.

With a shock, Jorna remembered her brother. "Eskil. Where is he?"

Kaysar bit her lip and looked down at the running boards. "I'm sorry to tell you this, Jorna, but he... didn't make it."

The panic came roaring back, the darkness too, as Commander Kaysar explained he must have passed out when he hit the water, which is why they couldn't get to him in time. The scent of jasmine settled over Jorna as the commander produced a silk handkerchief from one of her uniform's pockets. "Here."

"What?" Jorna stared at it uncomprehendingly, then the breeze stirred, chilling her cheeks, wet once more, this time with tears. For her brother. For herself. For how close they'd come to losing everything. She tightened her hold on Ava's hand. At least she still had this. "Thanks."

"Thank *you*." Kaysar gave her a watery smile. "You did everything you could. Never forget that."

11

"WHY DID HE do it?" Lieutenant Goh asked, the only person on board brave or foolish enough to break the silence as the skiff made its way back to the hangar.

From her seat on the back bench with the med tech still hovering over her, Jorna forced herself to answer the man. "Jump, you mean?"

Goh nodded. There was frustration in his pinched expression but also a need to understand just what happened.

That made two of them.

Jorna blew out a breath. She supposed his question was valid since he was one of the people who helped fish her out of the ocean. "My guess is he knew he would be going home in disgrace. In his mind, he'd sacrificed his soul for this mission and was no longer worthy of any type of salvation." That he would be taking her with him was an added bonus. "A trial would only further hurt his cause and garner scrutiny of the Supplicants."

"There should be some of that anyway," Goh grumbled.

Jorna agreed but doubted it would be enough to fully root out such extremism. Forcing it back into hiding was the best they could hope for.

Commander Kaysar, leaning against the skiff railing, watched on while the tech finished up. Her hands were fists at her sides as if she had to restrain herself from reaching out. "I want you fully checked out by Dr. Rafa as soon as we get back."

The logistics of that rebooted the analytical part of Jorna's brain. "How did you manage to get over here anyway?"

"We loaded everyone into one of the transports and entered through the habitat's exterior hangar." The same one they used to deliver the plants to the mainland weeks ago.

"My brother had a partner in all this as well?"

Kaysar nodded. "One of Dr. Rafa's med techs. We think that's how they got ahold of your DNA so easily." The med tech trainee? That would certainly explain the weirdness with her botched IV port at her last appointment.

"So I'm no longer a person of interest in this case?"

The commander tipped her head as she considered that. "No, but there will be questions and reports and so forth." No doubt they'd both be drowning in documentation over this ordeal for a long time.

"Still. Thank you for believing me, even when you had no reason to. I don't know what I would have done otherwise."

Commander Kaysar's mouth pinched together as if she wanted to argue with that assertion. Instead, she said, "I'm sorry for your loss."

A bitter chuckle escaped Jorna, and she couldn't blame it

on getting zapped. Or drowned for that matter. "I lost my family a long time ago. And a whole lot more. But at least we didn't lose the Climasphere."

Kaysar nodded, giving the habitat one last glance as Goh directed the skiff into the hangar. "But we're going to have to go over this place with a fine-tooth comb to ensure your brother didn't leave any more surprises behind."

The skiff passed through the hangar's electrostatic barrier, and the docking clamps locked on a moment later.

"Plus all the damage." Jorna could just imagine all the sensor alerts and warnings they'd tripped throughout the habitat today. Not to mention the repairs the electroculture gradient would need. They had a lot of work to do. "And Savvy?"

Kaysar gave her a reassuring smile as Goh and the others disembarked. "Your assistant will be patched up in one of our workshops as soon as possible. It kept us in the loop just like you asked it to."

Jorna nodded and got to her feet. Now that they were alone, there was only one thing left to do. "Then I'd like to formally offer my resignation." She didn't see how she could do otherwise, considering all the trouble she'd caused through her refusal to talk about her past. Perhaps this way she'd be able to claw back a few shreds of professionalism in the process. "Dr. Li will no doubt be well equipped to pick up where—"

Kaysar stood tall. "Absolutely not."

Jorna reared back, surprised by Kaysar's sharp tone. "But she's the best person for the job." As much as it killed Jorna to say it, it was true now more than ever.

The commander held up a hand for silence. "I'll not hear

another word. As far as I'm concerned, your actions today not only saved the sphere from destruction but demonstrated your commitment to everything we've built here. The only person you need to convince of that is yourself."

Jorna shook her head. "If you won't grant me this, then I'll go to the Climate Action Council directly."

"I'll make it so the only thing anyone's granting you is medical leave," Kaysar promised her.

Jorna swiped at her eyes. She would not cry again today. But why was the commander making this so difficult?

Kaysar took a step toward her. "Don't you see? What you need is time, Jorna. After what you've been through, you shouldn't be making any big decisions. About your career, about your future…"

"About you?" Jorna challenged.

Kaysar gave her a sad smile. "About me too. But I'll be here when you're—"

"Ready?" Jorna crossed her arms, furious at being denied her request, at being denied the one thing she'd wanted for herself, at being countermanded even if it *was* for her own good. "Well, don't worry. I wouldn't want to distract you from your responsibilities around here since that's all you seem to care about."

Kaysar's face wavered, then smoothed out into an impersonal mask. "Report to Dr. Rafa's office," she told Jorna, like she was any other staff member. The shift was a shock to the system and just as devastating, even though part of Jorna knew she deserved it. "And that's an order."

ACCELERATED GROWTH ENVIRONMENT

AFTER DR. RAFA gave Jorna a clean bill of health, she was required to undergo a week of intensive therapy with one of the resident psychiatrists on board. She kept going, two times a week, mostly to keep the nightmares at bay as she fielded inquiries from the authorities about Eskil and prepared report after report for funding agencies, insurance companies, and their partnering institutions. She had one video call with Karin when they finally anchored off the coast of the Dominican Republic where she tried to explain everything that had happened in the habitat that day, but Jorna had to cut it short when Karin asked Jorna to pray with her. If this situation had taught her anything, it was to not to let her past hurt her more than it already had.

And that meant making hard choices about who she let into her life going forward.

Once Jorna had gotten through the bulk of the paperwork, she resumed her duties, eager to get a handle on which specimens had thrived during her absence, and which ones needed extra support despite the best efforts of the horticulture techs in training. She also spent a good chunk of her time helping Meigs to undo the damage her brother had wrought on the habitat. Every day, Jorna could focus a little bit longer on the task at hand, but the rest of the time it was as though she was trapped in the fog that frequently enveloped the tropical rainforest tier. Everything felt fuzzy, almost unreal, as she went through the motions while her mind churned.

It wasn't grief. It wasn't boredom. It was Commander Ava Kaysar.

Even though Jorna had only the briefest of interactions

with the commander over the last few weeks, she still lingered in her mind. No longer merely a distraction, but a fundamental part of her life she was unwilling to relinquish.

"Hey, Doc—"

Her therapist said it was time to reach out, but Jorna still felt a mixture of anger and shame whenever she thought about the last time they spoke. The commander had only been trying to help Jorna, even though she wasn't in a place where she could accept that for the gift it was at the time. Now, Kaysar invaded her thoughts, her memories, and every contingency Jorna was capable of conjuring, and she could no longer use her past as an excuse.

Now you get to decide who you are without the weight of such a history holding you back.

Jorna knew what she wanted, what she was afraid to want, but that didn't matter if Commander Kaysar didn't—

"—hand me that magnadriver, would you?"

Meigs's voice was a shock as the Hive hummed around them. Rotors shuttled drones in and out of the massive cargo bay for their scheduled tasks. There was so much energy traveling through miles of conduit and wires in here, Jorna's skin prickled.

"Hmm?" she blinked, slow to focus on where the chief engineer had a spot irrigator splayed open on a worktable.

"Never mind. I got it." Meigs used the magnadriver to reattach the drone's CPU cover, then double-checked the readout on her touchscreen. "That should be the last of them," she said with no little pride. "A clean bill of health."

Jorna struggled to match her enthusiasm. "Glad to hear it."

"And with the exception of that one bomb with the faulty

wiring we found in the lab, the sphere's clean as well." Meigs made a point to look behind Jorna. "You don't have any other siblings stashed around here, do you?"

"Not on board at least." Commander Kaysar had made sure of that much.

Meigs slapped her shoulder as they walked out of the Hive. "Thank *god* for that."

The quip cut a bit too close to the bone for Jorna's tastes, but Meigs didn't notice or didn't care. And considering how closely they'd worked together over the course of the harvest, Jorna was grateful her brother's actions hadn't changed the dynamic between them.

If only the same thing could be said of everyone else.

Savvy was in the wall charger but flashed to life when Jorna returned to the lab. "Dr. Benton, new results on the efficacy of phytochemical-driven irrigation have come in."

Her assistant had been put back to rights, thanks to the Climasphere's engineers, in record time. Newly printed components had been installed, and Savvy got a new coat of matte silver paint that only a factory representative could tell was a shade off from the original.

"Thanks, Savvy. Has Commander Kaysar responded to my message?"

"Not this one or the five others you've sent this week."

New paint, but the same old Savvy underneath.

"Glad to know you're keeping track," Jorna grumbled under her breath. Keeping track of things was one of Savvy's primary functions, of course, but they still had to calibrate what things needed emphasis and which ones were best left unsaid.

"Your next gene therapy appointment with Dr. Rafa is

tomorrow. Perhaps while you're over there, you could speak to the commander."

Now even Savvy was pushing her to reach out. Jorna just grunted as she picked up a touchscreen and scanned the results set. But she couldn't focus on the graphs and charts. She couldn't focus on anything in the habitat, not when what she was fixated on was most likely on the Bridge. "What's Commander Kaysar's schedule like for the rest of the day?"

"Her shift on the Bridge does not end for another hour. Her calendar indicates she is free until a security briefing at oh-eight-hundred hours tomorrow morning."

"Any other pressing business I need to handle around here?"

"Not at the moment, Dr. Benton."

"Then I'll see you in the morning."

Without giving herself the option to turn back, Jorna headed for the shuttle. The repaired corridor still smelled of solder, grease, and off-gassing plastic, but it felt reassuringly solid underfoot as she crossed over. She kept her head as empty as possible of second thoughts and spiraling what-ifs as the shuttle brought her to the executive sector.

"Dr. Benton on the Bridge," the comms officer announced as she entered.

Lieutenant Goh turned around in the hot seat and gave Jorna a surprised look. "Doctor, how can we help you?"

The bland inquiry, for once not simmering with banked hostility, should have cheered Jorna, but she breezed right over that when she realized Commander Kaysar wasn't there. "I'm sorry to interrupt, but I was hoping to find—"

The door to the attached conference room opened,

admitting Commander Kaysar and her navigation officer. The officer went to his workstation. The commander wiped the momentary surprise from her features as she focused on Jorna. "Dr. Benton, I hope all's well with the habitat."

Jorna straightened. "Yes, but I do have an update for you." She gestured to the hall. "On the, um, drones."

"The drones? I see." Kaysar nodded to her second. "Lieutenant, you have the Bridge." Her expression gave nothing away as she joined Jorna in the hall.

For a moment, all Jorna could do was indulge in the commander's presence, the bun at the nape of her neck messy from fiddling, the blue of her eyes vibrant though she didn't quite meet her gaze. The only thing missing was that smile of hers.

Jorna clamped down on her professionalism even as anticipation filled her. "I came to tell you Meigs has ensured every last drone in the Hive is now clear of tampering."

"And I was glad to hear it when she made her report, oh, about twenty minutes ago."

"Oh." That would have been right around the time Jorna made her decision to head over.

Commander Kaysar raised her brows. "Is there something you'd like to add, Doctor?" A courteous question, considering they both knew Jorna had fabricated an excuse to see her.

Jorna swallowed, her mouth suddenly dry. "Only to commend Chief Engineer Meigs and those on loan for going above and beyond in this particular matter."

Kaysar nodded. "I'll make sure to mention that in my

report. Anything else?" She sounded perfectly agreeable, almost blasé, but missing the spark that had always marked her personality.

Jorna wanted it back. She wanted a lot of things when it came to the commander, but perhaps that most of all. Jorna cleared her throat. "Yes. I'm looking for something. Perhaps you can help me find it."

"What is it?"

"The version of you when we first met. Where is she?" Jorna said it so quickly, she feared Kaysar would miss the reference.

But she blinked rapidly and finally met Jorna's gaze with a jolt of blue. "Her? Oh, well, a lot has happened since then, hasn't it. I wasn't sure it was the right time for her to return."

Jorna's ribs squeezed. "Understandable, given what happened, but if it wouldn't be too much trouble, could you let her know that it was never her that was the problem? It was me. But now..."

Commander Kaysar lifted her chin. "Now?"

"I don't want my past to take anything else from me. We almost lost the Climasphere. I don't want to lose whatever this is with you—her—too."

Kaysar dipped her head. "I think I understand. I'll... let her know."

"Thank you." Jorna turned to go, not wanting to push her luck.

"It may take some convincing," the commander called after her.

Jorna stopped, turned, grateful to see the first hint of a smile on Kaysar's face. "You have any advice for me?"

She tipped her head, considering. "For starters, a full-throated apology."

Jorna took a step toward her, knowing she had to get this right. "I'm prepared to grovel," she said solemnly.

"Then there are practical matters to see to. Ground rules, expectations, calendar permissions…"

"Naturally."

Kaysar's blue eyes darkened as Jorna stood before her, close enough to breathe in her perfume, to touch her again if she dared. "Negotiations could be quite intense. Are you sure you're up for it?"

"I've fully recovered from my injuries, if that's what you mean."

Kaysar bit her lip, holding back a grin. "I was thinking emotionally, but that's, ah, also good to know." She paused invitingly for a moment. "In fact—"

Jorna's wristcom squealed with a priority message. "Dr. Benton," Savvy's voice cut in. "Your vital signs have become erratic. Are you having a medical emergency? Would you like me to alert—"

"Not now, Savvy," she said tersely. "Everything's fine. Benton, out."

Kaysar chuckled. "Then there's the matter of your hardware…"

"Savvy and I will have a little chat."

"No more chaperones?"

"No," Jorna agreed. "No more running away. No more hiding."

Kaysar arched a brow. "No more secrets?"

"I don't have any left. Does this mean I can kiss you now?"

"Hmm." Kaysar crossed her arms in mock seriousness, chin in hand. "We should probably try to do things properly this time."

"Anything," Jorna said. And meant it.

"How about we start with a stroll through the habitat?"

Jorna grinned at the thought, for once no what-ifs churning through her. "That can certainly be arranged. I hear the tiger lilies are blooming."

"I heard that rumor too. It would make for a fresh start."

Jorna took Ava's hand in hers. A fresh start to an even brighter future. "Together."

ACKNOWLEDGMENTS

MUCH LIKE THE construction of the Climasphere, the creation of a book is never a lone endeavor. Many people are needed to coax an idea into existence and help see it through to its final, printed form. I am so grateful to my family, friends, and colleagues for joining me on yet another publishing journey with *Accelerated Growth Environment*.

This book would not have been possible without the support of my husband Eric and my daughter Brynn. I wish to thank them for always giving my writing the space and encouragement it needs to grow. Your love keeps me going each day I put pen to paper.

Thanks also to Curtis C. Chen, Christopher East, Chris Gerwell, Brian D. Hinson, Kelly Lagor, Sara A. Mueller, Rae Oestreich, Rebecca Roanhorse, Ian Tregillis, Sarena Ulibarri, and Fran Wilde for their feedback on an earlier version of this book.

Finally, I wish to thank Brianne Shiraki and Josh Sutphin for taking such care with this project from start to finish. I am honored *Accelerated Growth Environment* is the first publication for Shiraki Press. Thanks to them, we will have even more stories of hopeful futures so we never forget what could one day be possible for all of us. I hope you find those same dreams for the future on the pages of not only this book but all the others to come from this press.

Thank you for reading.

Photo by Kim Jew Photography Studios

LAUREN C. TEFFEAU was born and raised on the East Coast, educated in the South, employed in the Midwest, and now lives and dreams in the Southwest. When she was younger, she poked around in the back of wardrobes, tried to walk through mirrors, and always kept an eye out for secret passages, fairy rings, and messages from aliens. She was disappointed. Now, she writes to cope with her ordinary existence.

Her work focuses on environmental issues, examines the role of technology in our lives, and centers women's voices through fantastical adventures and immersive worlds. Her novel *Implanted* (2018, Angry Robot) was a finalist for the 2019 Compton Crook award for best first SF/F/H novel and named a definitive work of climate fiction by Grist. Her environmental fantasy novella *A Hunger With No Name* was published by the University of Tampa Press in 2024. Over twenty of her short stories have appeared in venues like *Sunday Morning Transport*, *DreamForge Magazine*,

After Dinner Conversation, and the Stoker Award-nominated *Chromophobia: A Strangehouse Anthology by Women in Horror*.

When not writing, she enjoys spending time with her family as well as biking, hiking, and learning aikido.

CONTRIBUTORS

Written by Lauren C. Teffeau

LAURENCTEFFEAU.COM

Edited by Brianne Shiraki

SHIRAKIPRESS.COM

Copyedited by Rachel Oestreich
The Wallflower Editing

THEWALLFLOWEREDITING.COM

Cover illustration by Stephan Martiniere

MARTINIERE.COM

Book design by Josh Sutphin

SHIRAKIPRESS.COM

This book was created entirely by humans.
No generative AI was used for any part of its production.

www.ingramcontent.com/pod-product-compliance
Lightning Source LLC
LaVergne TN
LVHW040148080526
838202LV00042B/3073